*The Great War. The waste and the futility of it*
*as summed up in this poem by Tony Brown,*
*who kindly gave me permission to use it as a leader to*
**Blitz & Pie~~**

## ...to end all

GW00630786

They called it The
The war to end
If only that w(
I'll give you a few
Maybe some you already knew

Eight and half million soldiers killed
Nine million civilians too
Twenty million wounded
These just the ones we knew

A whole generation of young men and boys
Wiped out and discarded like broken toys
In one battle alone sixty thousand men slain
And that was on just the first day
Nearly two million shells were fired in vain
And that was on just the first day

Life in the trenches was beyond all belief
Two weeks at a stretch without any relief
Up to their ankles in deep mud and water
Then over the top to engage in the slaughter

But on one Christmas Day the guns ceased their chatter
They decided that one day of peace wouldn't matter
They came out of their holes to sing carols and chat
They played football, yes, football
How crazy was that
They gave gifts to each other as brother to brother

But the following day they were killing each other
Does this not inform us how futile is war
When men can kill men
They made friends with before
Simply because it is all one can do
If you don't kill the enemy he will kill you

If we would strife to justify the killing and the pain
It can only be by lessons learned to not go there again
The war to end all wars it was supposed to set us free
A very sobering thought indeed but it was not to be

Just twenty one years later it all begun again
And millions more from every side
gave up their lives in vain

Why should any race or creed be made to follow orders
To maim and kill their fellow man
And invade each other's borders

Another conflict, thousand dead
Woman and children in their beds
Beautiful cities left to burn...
When will we learn

Why can't we share resources
That are found upon this earth
Then everyone around the world
would be of greater worth
Why can't we live our own lives,
not interfere with others
Maybe then and only then
there'll be far fewer
Grieving mothers.

Tony Brown august 2014

## Dedication

*Chat*

To all the friends and acquaintances we got to know in the period of this book, although we have all gone our separate ways, we hope life has been good for you and we wish you well.

Percy W. Chattey

# BLITZ & PIECES

AUSTIN MACAULEY
PUBLISHERS LTD.

A CIP catalogue record for this title is available from the British Library.

Information used from elsewhere and additions are in the public domain others I have made every effort to acknowledge the original author of the items used if I have missed any person then I apologise as it was not by intention.

ISBN 978 1 78455 660 0 (Paperback)
ISBN 978 1 78455 662 4 (Hardback)

www.austinmacauley.com

First Published (2015)
Austin Macauley Publishers Ltd.
25 Canada Square
Canary Wharf
London
E14 5LB

Printed and bound in Great Britain

# Acknowledgments

*With grateful thanks and loads of love to
my dear wife Jean, and also to our
lovely growing family.*

*A very special thank you to Nicki Murphy for her
continued support and help.*

*Grateful thanks also to Derek Cook for the cover
design.*

The cover picture is part of a painting by an unknown artist and originates from the 1940s

Some songs reflect one's life the following suits mine!

I've been a puppet, a pauper, a pirate,
A poet, a pawn and a king.
I've been up and down and over and out
But I know one thing:
Each time I find myself flat on my face,
I pick myself up and get back in the race.

*With respect to Frank Sinatra's song 'That's Life'*

By the same Author:

**Motorway**
**Humpty Majority Sat on the Wall**
**Politically Incorrect**
**Who called Last Orders?**
**Living in Spain**
**The Black Venus**
**Death for a Starter**
**Watch*it!***
**Watch*it Too!***
**The Black Venus**

# Contents

# Pictures of the Bombing

*This is a true story of love, laughter and struggle: The struggle of surviving the bombing of London during the 1940s and then trying to find my way in the world after being brought up in very hard and difficult times in East London.*

*This story is full of anecdotes, some funny, others disastrous, but they are all true coming from a varied career and business life.*

*To give the reader a fuller picture of events some of the pictures and text explain in more detail of that time, and are thoughts or facts from other people's points of view in italics. Most of the items are taken off the Internet from Wikipedia (the free Encyclopaedia) for which I'm grateful.*

*Other pictures are taken from my own albums and records of events, unfortunately, some have faded over time.*

# Foreword - The Shelter

*The 'Blitz' from the German word 'Lightning'*

It was a bitterly cold, damp night and there was a clammy, musty smell in the confined space. Water which had formed from condensation was running down in rivulets from the corrugation of the steel walls and ceiling. The wetness was finding its way into the tiny cramped bed I was lying on, with sparse covering.

Outside, where we were trying to sleep, there was the constant drone of the engines from the German Bombers who were thundering the ground with their bombardment of heavy explosives. Some of the bombs being dropped weighed over a ton. They had been doing this every night for many months.

The ground was constantly shaking with the continuous bombing. Adding to the noise was our fighter planes who were weaving in and out of the night sky attacking the endless flow of enemy bombers who were determined to destroy everything in their path.

Lying on the hard bunk beds, we would hear on occasions a thump of an explosion, and then another a little closer followed by a further five or six, each one getting nearer and nearer. I would curl up tight in a ball fully expecting the next one would be the one which would hit us. The sound was deafening − the shelter shook, causing the water droplets to fall from the ceiling. As the colossal noise died away Father would take the chance of being hit by falling shrapnel and go outside to see if the house, about twenty yards away was still standing.

In the morning when the all clear sounded, we would leave the cold damp hole and with cramped legs stumble through the narrow opening up the makeshift steps into the garden. After the cold of the night and now the silence, although the noise of the dark hours still ringing in our heads, it all seemed unreal as nothing had changed, with the exception of pieces of sharp metal from the shells and bombs that had exploded lying around the garden and in the streets.

As soon as we arrived in the house Father would, like most of our neighbours tune into the BBC News to hear of the night's events – what follows is a true sample of one of their bulletins:

## BBC News Broadcast September 1940:

**London blitzed by German bombers** The German Air Force has unleashed a wave of heavy bombing raids on London, killing hundreds of civilians and injuring many more. The Ministry of Home Security said the scale of the attacks was the largest the Germans had yet attempted. "Our defences have actively engaged the enemy at all points," said a communiqué issued this evening. "The Civil Defence services are responding admirably to all calls that are being made upon them."

The first raids came towards the end of the afternoon, and were concentrated on the densely populated East End, along the river by London's docks. About 300 bombers attacked the city for over an hour and a half. The entire docklands area seemed to be ablaze as hundreds of fires lit up the sky. Once darkness fell, the fires could be seen more than 10 miles away, and it is believed that the light guided a second wave of German bombers which began coming over at about 2030 BST (1930 GMT).

The night bombing lasted over eight hours, shaking the city with the deafening noise of hundreds of bombs falling so close together there was hardly a pause between them.

One bomb exploded on a crowded air raid shelter in an East London district.

In what was described as "a million to one chance", the bomb fell directly on the 3ft (90cm) by 1ft (30cm) ventilation shaft − the only vulnerable place in a strongly-protected underground shelter which could accommodate over 1,000 people.

About 14 people are believed to have been killed and 40 injured, including children.

Civil Defence workers worked through the night, often in the face of heavy bombing, to take people out of the range of fire and find them temporary shelter and food.

An official paid tribute to staff at one London hospital which was hit, saying, "They showed marvellous bravery, keeping on until bomb detonations and gunfire made it absolutely impossible."

In the air, a series of ferocious dogfights developed as the German aircraft flew up the Thames Estuary.

The Air Ministry says at least 15 enemy aircraft crashed into the estuary, and in all, the Ministry said, 88 German aircraft were shot down, against 22 RAF planes lost.

This incredible picture was taken during a German air raid in 1940. It shows British and German contrails high in the skies above our capital as the brave boys of the RAF fought to save the lives of the innocent Londoners below them, with the Luftwaffe readied to release their bombs.

***With grateful thanks for the above picture to 'Friends United.'
To become a member go to www.friendsunited.com***

# The Early Years

During the First World War 1914 – 1918, Hitler, who was to have a big effect on my life, was a dispatch riding corporal in the German Army travelling around the trenches carrying orders to the troops which had been issued by their superiors. Sixteen years later in 1934 he was Germany's leader as Chancellor, a dictator and in control with a desire to conquer Europe.

*Adolf Hitler, on the left, a cross over his head, with a group of German Soldiers in the First World War (from Wikipedia).*

It was the following year in early October 1935 when there was a lot of screaming going on at the Hospital, situated next to Blackwall Tunnel in East London. (The hospital has since been demolished.)

The noise in the Poplar Hospital was me arriving into the world. The hospital is within the sound of Bow Bells, which traditionally makes me a true cockney famous for its rhyming slang, although I have never fully understood how sometimes it is interpreted. In fact most of it is made up by individuals when talking to make a point about something by rhyming the major word with something quite different. The most famous in folk law is *Apple and pears* meaning stairs. But I have never heard it used − it normally got shortened to *The apples*, it is really all part of the Cockney sense of humour.

I was the second child after Frances, who was born in June 1932.

The Poplar Hospital, at that time, was one hundred years old having been built in 1835, and was situated near the gates of the East London Docks. Its original purpose was for dock employees and seamen who needed medical attention, and I guess its facilities were a bit basic.

There are no ships in the docks today. When containers were developed which could be loaded onto ships for moving goods around the world, the London Docks became obsolete as they were too small for the large vessels and unloading facilities needed for the new resource. This type of ship started to discharge and collect their cargoes from ports that had the new supply and were large enough to accommodate them. Today the old docks have a different use. Most of the warehouses have gone and have been replaced with towering blocks of offices and luxury flats, whilst the waterways have become marinas and used for other leisure facilities.

My parents shared, with my grandparents a rented, small, two-storey end of terrace house which had been built in the Victorian period, at the bottom of Saville Road. The property was near the railway line which separates Chadwell Heath from the rest of Dagenham.

The house was insignificant and cramped inside with an outside W.C., and there was no electricity: Lighting in the evening was by a gas fitting on the wall which had a very delicate filament which needed a flame put to it for it to light. Bath time was maybe once a week, in a galvanised tin tub which, when not in use, hung outside on the wall. On bath nights it would be brought inside and put in front of the fire and was filled with jugs of hot water. There was no change of liquid between individual baths it was just topped up at intervals with water out of a hot kettle. Washing machines, fridges and white goods were not heard of; if they were, they were out of reach of our family money wise.

As a toddler my favourite pastime was to slide down the railway embankment to the gravel road just outside the back door of the house, as I remember we used something akin to a tin tray. I say *we* because there were two of us, but I do not remember the name of the other person, in fact I am not sure if I ever knew what he was called. What I do remember was he lived a few doors along the road from us.

From time to time in my activity of sliding down the bank, I would scratch or cut myself and as the ground was of loose shale there was sometimes dirt around the damaged part. Gran would say 'Don't be a cry baby, it will get better and a little bit of dirt won't hurt you.' A big difference from today's attitude – recently in Spain I was in A&E with a friend who was very ill, so ill we thought we were going to lose him. There was a young couple full of giggles because he had scratched his knee. If they thought it was that funny why were they taking up valuable hospital space and time. I digress.

Opposite where we lived at the end of Saville Road there were large playing fields with the railway running beside them. I was banned from that area, although later, when I was at senior school our sports days were held there. Today I believe it is used by the East London, West Ham Football Club for training.

The railway belonged to L.N.E.R. *(London & North Eastern Railways)* which was nationalised in the late 1940s to become part of British Rail. The large, normally black, sometimes dark green, steam engines would scream past pulling express carriages, their wheels going 'did did did da' as they went over the expansion joints in the rails, all heading for the towns further into Essex and beyond. There were also local *chuggers*, stopping at each station. Trains were very frequent billowing smoke also coal soot out of their chimneys, even today sixty years on, one can see the soot marks on the bridges where the engines had expelled their exhaust. It was always a beautiful and exciting sight watching these monsters breathing smoke and steam as they went on their journey. I don't think watching the modern equivalent gives the same thrill.

As the trains went noisily past, there would be two men on the open platforms driving these huge machines. One would be wearing grey overalls and a peaked cap of the same colour, whilst looking after the controls to drive the locomotive with a small roof over his head. The other, the fireman covered in black dust and sweat, as he fed fuel from the attached coal tender to the fire which heated the water filled boiler, to create steam to keep the train moving. As they went speeding on their way they would wave to us youngsters, gazing in wonderment at them.

I remember one day it was frosty with an icy wind and I went through the small back yard to go indoors out of the chill. The front of the house was out of bounds, and I cannot remember it at all. As I went into the interior, which served as a kitchen and family room with lino on the floor, I was feeling very cold. I got the customary telling off from my apron clad grandmother, who used to look after me, for being dirty from sliding down the embankment.

I had gone inside moaning about my cold hands, she held them near the range, situated on the right hand side of the room. The stove supplied not only the heating for the house, although the heat did not get as far as the bedrooms, but also the cooking. This was done on its top hot plates with an oven below – all of which was heated by the coal fire. The whole object was a large black shining thing made of steel. The shine was where it had been cleaned and wiped over with heat proof Black Lead, a normal daily chore done by my grandfather. By opening its front door more heat would come out from the burning coals.

Grandma held my hands near the flames to warm them; as a result I got a severe case of chilblains. There was no cure other than an old remedy of rubbing juice from a cut potato on the affected part which gave little relief. The National Health Service would not be formed for another twelve or so years. Visiting the doctor or obtaining medicines was too expensive and when somebody was hurt the cure was by remedies that had been passed down over the years. In this instance, it was a case of just rubbing with the potato and waiting for the pain to go away.

One day there was great excitement in the family; Father had managed to convince the local authority that we were entitled to a rented council house, because we were two families living in cramped conditions with six people sharing two bedrooms. In those days very few people bought their own homes, it wasn't unheard of but it was unusual and the majority did exactly what we were going to do – rent.

Between the wars in the 1920s and '30s, to satisfy the demand for rented property, there were major building programmes of council houses. Large estates were being built, not only around London but also elsewhere. These modern day houses also replaced the terrible slums that had existed earlier in the century. The Becontree Estate in Dagenham, where building started in 1921, was the largest in Europe at that time. It was constructed to the South of Dagenham just a few miles from Chadwell Heath, and took more than eight years to complete. It coincided with the Ford Motor Company developing its large facility on the banks of the River Thames.

The great day arrived and a large ramshackle van appeared to move our furniture. Well it looked large to me as I was still a toddler of about two or three years old, and it was probably no bigger than a current day Transit, which would have been big enough, as we did not have many belongings.

At that time there was a popular music hall song, 'My old man said follow the van and don't dilly dally on the way.' It goes on to say 'dillied, I dallied and lost my way and can't find my way home'. The meaning of the song dates to the early part of the 20th century.

As already stated most people lived in rented property. At that time virtually all factory and dock work was piece work, which meant you were paid when you worked and what you produced, normally on a daily basis. If one didn't work then there was no money. The system was men would queue at the locked gates of the places of employment and the owners would decide how much labour they required that day. Sometimes it could be days or weeks before a person got chosen, so income would be sporadic and very short. Food would come first; the result: there was often not enough money for the rent. In those days it was a serious offence not to pay your rent and it could mean a prison term, so it was not unknown for families to do 'a moonlight flit', with nowhere to go they would have to search for somewhere to live.

Back to Saville Road, the van got loaded and off it went but there was no room for Mum and me, so we had to walk. I do not remember where my sister was but she would have been old enough to go to school, so perhaps that is why she was not with us. I also do not remember much about the walk to East Road which for small legs would have been a long way. But I do remember walking up Saville Road holding Mother's hand watching the van disappear in the distance. Mum was teasing me with the song and I remember being worried about where we were going, but as it turned out, both my mother and father knew exactly where we were to live and had visited the place sometime earlier.

On that day we walked in the centre of Saville Road, the pavements were too bad and not very level for walking. The roads were empty with no cars parked as very few people owned one, and as the road was a cul-de-sac, traffic was non-existent, so the centre of the road was quite safe.

Funny thing about life: it has a way of combining events many years apart. As an instance, at that time I could not have realised that twenty odd years later I would be courting Jean, the love of my life, my friend and soul mate, who would be living with her parents, a few streets away from that walk to our new home. Nor was I to know that on that day I would be walking past the house where, the other loves of my life, our two children, Anne and Sue, would be attending nursery school.

# East Road,
# Chadwell Heath

There were four roads named after the compass points: not only was there an East Road, there were also North, West and South Roads set in a quadrangle, which were tree-lined and with semi-detached, well kept council houses to each side with large rear gardens going to the centre of the four sides. The dwellings in the east of this arrangement and where we were to live were of a later period and a different design and probably only a few years old when we arrived.

East Road was a lot longer than the other three and ran from the Eastern Avenue to the north, which was a dual carriageway and one of the main eastern routes out of London. The road also ran parallel with Whalebone Lane to the east, which was the main route south to Dagenham Docks and the Ford Motor Company, a very large motor manufacturing plant on the side of the River Thames.

Chadwell Heath, which was part of the London Borough of Dagenham, was the eastern boundary of the built up part of London, to the east of which was the Green Belt: an area surrounding the capital where building development was forbidden.

I think it was early spring when Mum and I walked into what was to be my home for the next fifteen or sixteen years. Number 27 was impressive to my young mind. We went up some steps and in through the front door, which was a first for me. But after that I was, or I should say we were encouraged to walk down the side of the property and use the rear door from the rear garden.

Inside it was spacious to what I had known before. It also had a separate bathroom on the ground floor − much better than that old tin tub, and a W.C. inside the house, albeit in the passageway leading to the rear garden. There was no heat in the toilet and it would get very cold in the winter.

The bath only had cold water plumbed to it by a tap fixed to the wall above it. The hot water came from a coal-fired boiler standing in the corner with a chimney going up to the ceiling and no doubt to the roof. A fire was lit below, and as there was no tap above it, cold water was poured in the top of the boiler from a galvanised steel bucket. When the water was hot it was ladled out into the bath. The weekly washing was also done in it by scrubbing the clothes in suds in the top of it.

The kitchen was a mass of doors with very little space for any furniture. The big square deep white Butler sink was in one corner and in an opposite corner with the bathroom door in between was the gas cooker, no units or worktops. In another corner was a cupboard with concrete shelves to keep the food chilled during the hot weather, fridges were not an item which a normal family could afford.

To make more working space, Father made a table that folded down over the bath, it was made of wooden planks and he was very proud of what he had achieved. On bath nights, when the bath was in use, the table folded up against the wall where there was a clip to hold it in place.

During that period Mother used to do the family ironing using a pair of solid steel irons, which she heated in front of the fire burning in the grate under the boiler, alternating them so as one got cold whilst ironing, she would change it for the one being heated in front of the hot coals.

One day Mother and Father, who had been out on one of their shopping trips came home with a basic clothes iron with an electric filament inside, but it did not have a thermostat to control the heat. When it started to get too hot one switched it off, and when it started to cool it was switched back on again.

I think we had gone away to pick peas for a weekend, or it could have been some other produce, which the local farmer needed harvesting. My sister, who had been left behind by herself in the house, had decided to use this new device, to do some ironing on the table over the bath which was normally used for this purpose. No doubt she did not give it a thought about a need to control the heat of the appliance as she was used to the old irons cooling down when you left them. When she had finished, without switching the thing off, she went out and left it lying flat on Father's pride and joy of a folding table. The iron had plenty of time over the weekend and slowly scorched the wood of the table top, and by the time we had arrived home the next day it had made its way through the inch thick wood and was dangling in the bath, from a hole in the table exactly the shape of the flat surface of the iron, the surrounding wood was still smouldering with smoke drifting from it. By now the heat in the iron had gone off because the coin in the electric meter had expired.

In the passage that led to the garden, and under part of the stairs was the coal cellar. The coal would arrive on a horse drawn dray with a flat bed and sacks of fuel lined up on them. It was drawn by two huge shire horses that would paw the ground with their hooves while they impatiently waited to move on to the next delivery.

The Carter was a big man with coal dust smeared across his face; he wore a black coat with leather patches over his shoulders, dark-coloured trousers with boots and gaiters. He would pull the very heavy coal sack off the dray by its top and load it on to his shoulder.

Bent double with the weight, he would carry it up the path between the two houses, through the gate, into the rear garden, in through the back door and down the passage. There he would lean over and pour the coal over his shoulder into the cellar, causing a thick cloud of black dust to rise in the air clinging to the walls, and entering the adjoining kitchen.

There was a downside to all the houses burning coal to heat their homes, and for other uses like driving steam engines, when it burns, it creates soot which can cause thick fog – they were called 'pea-soupers' and caused many deaths especially in the elderly.' This is when the soot mixes with waterborne mist and does not escape into the upper air, the result is it is difficult to breathe and sight is limited to a few yards through the thick swirling mass. If you are out in it the black smudge gathers around your nose and mouth. It was not until after the war did Parliament bring in the Clean Air Act, which restricted the use of coal as a fuel, although you could buy a clean version which did not give off smoke.

Each house had its own front and rear garden, the one at the rear was very long and wide designed for the time when most people grew their own vegetables. There were government signs in all the busy places stating 'Dig for Victory' meaning grow your own food, and that is what the family set out to do.

The garden had many uses: it was a food store by growing vegetables, in addition keeping chickens and rabbits. It was also a haven from the German bombers because of the steel shelter that was to be built there. Above all, it was a playground, many enjoyable hours of playing 'make believe', building forts for toy soldiers, developing a pond with small fish which were caught in a net from the stream in the nearby field. Watching frogs grow from spawn into tadpoles, and finally watching their little legs form.

Inside the house I had my own bedroom; it was at the top of the stairs at the back of the house and overlooked the rear garden. When we first moved in the lighting at night was by gas. One wall light fitting on the top landing, nothing in the bedrooms as it was too dangerous, if the filament went out the fumes could kill you. It was a little while later that electricity was installed and then I had a central light in my room. And an electrical socket to plug things into.

This electrical system had been wired around the house and was fed from a supply coming in at the front door with a meter high on the wall, which one had to put money in to make the thing function.

One afternoon I was upstairs with my brother playing some game when we smelt smoke. Opening the bedroom door, smoke was pouring up the stairs, and flames were coming from the meter. We were trapped; there was no way out. How my father put the flames out − I do not know as eventually we could not see down the stairs, but luckily he had called in home, saw what was happening, and managed to restore order. It was some time later that my mother told us that her father had died in a fire when she was about seven years old, by being trapped upstairs when a fire broke out on the ground floor.

Today when visiting other homes or staying in hotels and the like, I still always ensure there is an escape route. A few Christmas's ago we were staying at an old farmhouse in France which was built with a lot of timber in its construction. The bedroom which was allocated to us was in the attic at the top of a stairway, at the bottom of which was the place with the highest fire risk, the kitchen. We would need to pass it as it was the only way out. We asked to change the rooms and were given one on the ground floor.

Let us go back to East Road. A few weeks after we arrived in our new home, the Council sent some men to decorate the house, the walls were to be painted and there was a choice of either green and cream or brown and cream. Mum and Dad chose the green for the bottom half of the walls and the top part in cream. There was no charge for this work.

One of the first memories I have of living in East Road was on a sunny day and Dad was cutting the lawn in the rear garden with a mower which had to be pushed back and forth, no electric power. He had stopped to talk to one of the neighbours: a Mr Walters, who lived at number 29. The two men were talking about the war and they mentioned peace and how it had not lasted very long. I knew what war meant because it was on everyone's lips, but peace?

When Dad stopped talking to our neighbour, he started pushing the mower with me riding on the handle with my feet placed where it splayed out at the bottom. I asked him what peace meant and he said it is the time between wars and no doubt there was going to be another one. What he said to my young mind almost explained it.

In the living room, which was called the front room, Father had a crystal set, which was a small, silver crystal with shining diamond like spots. It was fitted on a wooden base and it had a small thin wire, called a cats whisker, which when it touched the crystal you could receive radio signals. Dad would listen through head phones, moving the wire around until he found the BBC Home Service, which was first broadcast in the 1920s and much later renamed Radio Two.

It was around about the start of the war when Mum and Dad bought a wireless set so we could all listen to the programmes. It was a big tan-coloured unit with a curved top, a dial on the front, with a grill for the speakers and four knobs to adjust the sound and to search for stations; it was sitting on its own homemade, black, rickety table in the corner of the room. When something interesting was being broadcast, neighbours, who had no such facility, would come in and it would be totally quiet in the room as everyone sat listening to the set.

The power for the radio was from two accumulators, which stored low voltage electricity like a battery. They were about half the size of a modern day car battery but had a glass case with a carrying handle to the top, and needed to be recharged every so often. The only way to do that was to take them down to the High Street; about twenty minutes walk away, where there was a shop that did this work. The units were heavy so we wheeled them down on an old pram.

Television in the late thirties was just being developed with the first broadcast being made from Alexandra Palace in North London. Very few people had a set, if they did, the programmes were not sent out very often, perhaps an hour a day. I did not know of such a thing until after the war.

On the 14th May 1939 my brother was born and the war started the following September.

# War is Declared

When the war was declared it was not a good day for anyone, everyone wondering what would happen? Would the Germans start bombing the next day as they did in the First World War? People sat round their wireless sets listening to the news which told us Germany had invaded Poland. Our government, a few days earlier, had put Hitler on notice that if his forces made such a move we would be at war with them. Most people were very frightened because they still had vivid memories of the millions that were killed and the horror of the thousands of casualties of the Great War 1914 – 1918, which had ended twenty one year's previously. Also people were frightened because some could remember how the Germans, in the First World War had sent bi-planes to bomb indiscriminately – minuscule to the Germans' ability in the nineteen thirties. Nobody had any knowledge of the horror of what was to come.

The following day dawned and nothing took place and the skies remained free of enemy aircraft. The relief, as everyone had been intense with worry and vivid memories of the previous war and the random bombing, all of which vanished in the morning light.

It was a few months later that I started my first school. I can remember very clearly my parents taking me for the first time to the Japan Road Infants School, housed in a very old Victorian building near to the High Road. I have always wondered why the small turning the school was off was named Japan Road, and what the significance was.

After that first introduction I was expected, and did, find my own way in the morning and afternoon, it was quite a long walk down a few roads and around Chadwell Heath Park. Although I had an elder sister I very rarely saw anything of her and where we lived our neighbours were mostly elderly with no children of my age so I got used to playing on my own.

Being born after September I started school in January, the middle of winter and bitterly cold. On arriving it was great to get there and have a warm in front of the big fire that would be burning in the main hall from a very old giant of a fireplace. When we, as children arrived, the fire would have a guard around it and on the hearth rows of milk in small bottles which would have been delivered that morning. If it was very cold they would have ice in the top of them on these mornings the school caretaker would line bottles up in front of the fire to warm the milk inside.

The large central hall, which had no side windows, natural light came from a large glass dome set in the ceiling, which was the roof of the building. The four classrooms, all lead directly off the hall, had no heating and whilst being taught we had to wrap up to keep the cold out. At break times we would get one of the free small bottles of milk, which in cold weather, as stated above, had been warmed in front of the fire.

I would walk to school in the morning, on my own. I had to make my way around the footpath that surrounded Chadwell Heath Park, it would be too early for the park keeper and the gates would be locked. After the day's lessons, the gates would be open and I could use the shortcut through the front gate of the park and down the paths between the pristine lawns to the far gate which was only a few streets from home. Sometimes I would get sidetracked and play with one of the children from school, which would delay me and trouble would be brewing for being late for tea.

The war had started and nothing appeared to be happening except the precautions against enemy attack. Gas masks were one item. I felt very lucky and proud because I had a grown up one. It was black, fitting tightly around my face. I felt proud because some others of my school peers had red Mickey Mouse ones with big black ears. My baby brother had a body gas repellent bag which he would be laid into and he could be seen through a clear glass window fitted into the closed top of the unit.

Thankfully the Germans did not use this terrible weapon of gas in any form. In later years, in the eighties, it was used by Iraqis against their neighbours − the Turks, with terrible effect many dying in the streets. In the First World War mustard gas was used by the Germans, against our troops in the trenches in France. This gas destroyed the lungs and killed thousands in a matter of minutes. The threat was frightening and very real.

As an extra, beside the gas masks, we also wore an arm band which, we were told, would turn yellow in the event of a gas attack; if that happened we should immediately put the mask on.

One day when I came home from school a large hole had been dug about halfway down our garden. I was told it was for the Anderson shelter, a couple of men were still there with their picks and shovels finishing off the work. The next day this silver corrugated iron oval thing stood out of the hole and the last of the steel sheets was being bolted to the front, leaving a small opening for the entrance which was down a few steps formed in the earth out of the surrounding ground. It was then that I was told, so as to protect against bomb blast it needed covering with the earth that had been dug out of the hole. So for the next hour or so, at the age of about five, that was my job.

There were other forms of bomb shelters, although the Anderson seemed to be the most popular. A school friend had what I now know as a Morrison. It was a brick built construction inside the house about the size of a large table and about the same height, which you had to crawl into but much more convenient than the shelters outside, at least you could get into it without walking down the garden in the cold or wet, in your night clothes.

About this time my grandparents moved from Saville Road, to The Close, which was a small cul-de-sac off East Road. They also had a long garden, the end of which passed the end of ours so a gate was installed, and we could then go back and forth to each other's houses without walking around the road.

It was on one of my visits to my grandparents, when I arrived she was cutting onions into two, and to my surprise she was putting them on the top shelf of the sideboard. I was a little taken back and asked why she had put them there. The answer was 'They keep the germs away,' and as my granddad died in his late eighties and Grandma in her middle nineties, at a time when the medical world was not as efficient as it is today, then perhaps there was something good in what she was doing. Needless to say, we still do buy big Spanish onions, cut them in two and lay them on the top shelf. Certainly Jean and I don't seem to suffer so many colds and sniffles like our peers. Oh and don't forget the garlic – it keeps the flies away!!

At the start of the war, Dad, and my uncle Bob, (*Dad's brother*) had two cars, which in itself was unusual as very few people owned even one. They were similar to the one shown on the next page: a 1936 Morris 8. It was very rare to see a car painted in anything other than *black* – I think it was Henry Ford that said 'You can have any colour providing it is black'. I digress. Petrol was severely rationed and could only be used for work that was involved in the war effort, and as at that time neither of them was, the cars had to be taken off the road. These two vehicles were put into store − other owners sold their vehicles to dealers who were prepared to store them to sell after the war. At that time most of the population believed that the conflict would be over very quickly.

Both the small vehicles owned by our family were pushed into Nan's rear garden for storage; there was just room to get them between the side of the house and the neighbour's fence. I had a great thrill because I was allowed to sit in one of them behind the steering wheel, not steering but I was fascinated by it. Perhaps that is where my interest in cars started.

As the differences between the two sides dragged on and Germany continued to invade most of the other European countries, the cars were disposed of as Grandma did not like them taking up most of her rear garden.

There was a lot of talk about the conflict but nothing appeared to be happening. It was decided by the government that children should be evacuated away from the dangers of bombs being dropped on London and other cities, but we children were not told of this arrangement.

One night I was woken up early and told to get dressed, so I got out of the warm bed into a bitterly cold bedroom. I was frightened I did not know what was happening and thought perhaps the Germans had arrived. It was just as cold downstairs as the fire in the living room, although still glowing from the previous evening, was not giving out very much heat. Outside it was pouring with rain and still dark, and we could hear the noise the water was making outside the house. Leaving home accompanied by both our parents we had to walk about a mile to Whalebone Lane School; where many years later I was to become a senior pupil.

In the playground were a line of cars, engines running and windscreen wipers sweeping back and forth. There were a lot of children all lined up carrying gas masks, boys in one line, wearing coats and short trousers with socks and shoes, the girls with similar footwear in another line but wearing dresses or skirts with coats over. We were all given a tag to tie on a lapel or button. I was not good at reading at that time so I do not know what it said but it was some form of identification.

After a little while, by now soaking wet because of the rain, we were directed to the cars. I remember being quite disappointed because I was put in a similar car to the one that I had sat in beside Nan's house, a Ford 8 or it could have been a Morris, they looked similar. I really wanted to go in the big car which was the one in front but other children were put into it.

Having said goodbye to my parents the cars started off in convoy and out of the gates. Inside the Ford/Morris it was cold and damp, the windows misting over with all our breathing and the damp clothes we had on. Basic vehicles did not have the luxury of heaters that was still a few years away. As we drove along, the driver was keeping the windscreen clear by wiping the moisture off with a cloth.

I was now going further than I had ever been before in my life, but worse it was with people I did not know and none of us had any idea where we were going or why. The cars hummed and rattled their way, going south, although at that time I did not know the meaning of south.

It was dark, each vehicle had coverings over their headlights so that the light would not spread and be seen from the air. There were no street lights, the shops and houses were in total darkness in compliance with the Blackout Laws. The rain was pouring down steadily making the journey very dark and slow.

We arrived at the Ford Motor Company, driving through the factory gates and down to Ford's Jetty which was built into the River Thames, as seen above with a ship tied up alongside it. I can remember the cars stopping beneath large cranes and we were told to get our things and to line up. Years later I was to drive on to that jetty many times.

It was very dark and outside lights were not allowed, because of the danger of enemy bombers lurking overhead. We were ushered onto a vessel, I do not know what sort of boat it was and was probably more of a ship, as by now I was too distressed and tired to take in what was going on. It must have been very early in the morning when we left the Ford jetty as it was still dark.

I do not remember much of the journey which would have been quite long going down the Thames and round the Essex and Suffolk coasts, because we finally arrived in Norfolk. I was not to know that at the time, it could have been anywhere and nobody was saying anything about our location. By a combination of train and bus we eventually arrived at a small coastal village early in the hazy morning light, where we lined up on the side of the street. Total strangers came along the line picking children and taking them away. *Can you imagine that happening today?*

I was near to last to be chosen and taken to a small terraced cottage near a railway bridge that crossed the road. I was very disappointed because other children had gone off in pairs, and I was on my own. I do not remember very much other than the lady was nice. If she had a husband he was probably away at the war. The thing that really struck me when I arrived was the small living room with the front door opening straight onto the street, which I thought was very strange. There was a tall cupboard door in the living room, again I was surprised because when she opened it the stairs started immediately, ours in East Road had a passage and a front door before you got to the stairs. We went up to the next floor and she showed me to what was to be my room. I did not like it; my personal things were still back in East Road.

I also remember being totally traumatised by being taken away from where we lived, not understanding what was happening and why I was living in this strange house with no family and a bedroom which was nothing like my one at home. For some reason the period I spent in Norfolk, is not very clear, I don't think I was very happy, strange people with a strange brogue, I felt out of place and badly wanted to go home.

After about six months or so, I was told that I was being sent home this time by train. It was many years later, when I thought about that period, I could not understand why we were sent to Norfolk by boat, when there must have been a big risk that the Germans could have attacked the ship and sunk it. Sadly this did happen to a ship which was taking children to be evacuated to Canada, with the loss of most of the people on board.

During the evacuation period I do not remember where my sister Fran was, I am sure she must have been sent away at the same time as me, but I do not remember, and I do not know where she went.

**Evacuation The following paragraphs taken from Wikipedia.**

*There was a steady flow of evacuees during June 1939. The official evacuation was declared on August 31, but began on September 1, two days before the declaration of war. From London and the other main cities, the priority class people boarded trains and were dispatched to rural towns and villages in the designated areas. With the uncertainties over registering for evacuation, the actual movement was also disjointed −evacuees were gathered into groups and put on the first available train, regardless of its destination. School and family groups were further separated in the transfer from mainline trains to more local transport. Accordingly, some reception areas became overwhelmed. East Anglian ports received many children evacuated from Dagenham. Some reception areas received more than the expected number of evacuees and others found themselves receiving people from a priority group or social class different from what they had prepared for.*

*Almost 3.75 million people were displaced, with around a third of the entire population experiencing some effects of the evacuation. In the first three days of official evacuation, 3.5 million people were moved −827,000 children of school-age, 524,000 mothers and young children (under 5), 13,000 pregnant women, 7,000 disabled persons and over 103,000 teachers and other 'helpers'. Host keepers were often put to inconvenience, especially by many children who seemed to be vulnerable to stress symptoms such as* <u>enuresis</u> *(bed wetting) and other ailments.*

# The Phoney War

Since the Victorian times in the 1800s, and even as late as the 1930s, in some families, and ours was one of those, boys and girls were not allowed to mix, not only going to separate schools but also having friends only of the same sex. I think this is still true in some parts of the United Kingdom.

At home my sister always had a separate room. When it was bitterly cold, the only heat in the house came from the coal fire in the living room, Bob and I would have to wait in the cold kitchen while our sister got ready for bed in the warmth, and after she had gone up to a cold bedroom and a freezing cold bed. Then it was our turn.

Sometimes to warm the bed Mum would boil a kettle to fill a hot water bottle which when pushed to the bottom of the covers kept your feet warm, but somewhere during the night it would go cold and then I used to curl my feet up out of its way.

My mother Frances was a Catholic, coming to England from Ireland when she was a small girl. In East Road she was still practising her faith. On occasions when the priest called to see her we had to hide upstairs as he did not know Mum was married with children, although at that time we had no idea who the visitor was. If he had known Mum was married he would not have recognised the union as it had not been blessed in the Catholic Church.

Mum must have been under terrible strain trying to keep her faith and deceiving her priest. Quite strange really, as by then, my parents had been married for almost eight years and Mum had kept it quiet from the church. It would be a long time before I understood any of this.

I never knew my grandparents on my mother's side, as her father had died in the aforementioned fire when she was very young. We never saw her mother who was never mentioned, perhaps that is because she had married outside the church.

My father was very Victorian in his ways and attitude. He was Church of England but did not attend services, which caused some conflict between him and Mother, especially more so in that my paternal grandmother was Jewish, although her husband, my grandfather, was not. I don't think that made for happy families; in that period people of different religions did not mix, and if you did, then you were seen as odd and were avoided, so it was kept secret. Please reader, do not take what I write as an insult to any religion or group of people.

The Victorians in the eighteen hundreds were very strict about moral codes. Females, wore their skirts normally at floor level. If they rose to show their ankles this was seen as very embarrassing. Even table legs and especially piano legs were covered so as not to cause offence.

My grandfather, on my father's side, was born in the late eighteen hundreds, and brought up in this period of restriction. His father, which would be my great grandfather, was a wealthy publican owning ten or more public houses in and around London, (go into Google and type 'Chattey Pubs') and would have followed the Victorian way of life.

My grandfather left home as a boy and joined the Army and was disowned by his family, which could have been because he married a Jewish girl. All this would explain why my father could be very strict as he was brought up shortly after that period. He could also be very unreasonable with a short temper; perhaps it was because he was one generation away from being wealthy. I do remember as a boy he would try and make contact with his father's family but was rebuffed.

** **

By the spring of 1940, hostilities had not spread to the home front, life had continued normally although there were restrictions like food rationing, and people were persuaded not to travel. Signs everywhere saying, 'Is your journey really necessary?'

About that time our troops were being rescued from Dunkirk. This event has been well documented in history when ships, and boats of all sizes, set off across the English Channel to rescue more than three hundred thousand men from the beaches of Western France

The first thing I noticed when I arrived back in East Road from the evacuation was all the trees along both pavements had been taken down and the road widened. The finish was in white concrete instead of the more pleasing black tarmac which it had been when I left. This changed the whole nature of the road from a little back water to an area waiting for something to happen.

I was told this was because if Whalebone Lane became unusable by a bomb destroying it, then the traffic could be diverted through our road to go to the important docks in Dagenham, my thought at the time was *but we have not seen any bombs.*

By that time Ford Motor Company was making military vehicles and the factory had been converted to war work, so there was a need to keep routes to these important facilities open. The use of our road as a diversion never happened but at times the bombs fell not far short of making it a possibility.

*The picture is of an Ack Ack gun from Wikipedia.*

\*\*

Before the war, a day out was to go pea picking. At about a mile from our house there was a farm in the north part of Whalebone Lane. It was always just getting light when we would arrive very early in the morning and climb onto the back of a lorry, as there were no seats we would hang on to the side as it travelled to its destination which would be a field awaiting to be harvested. On arrival we would alight from the vehicle clutching our lunch in a bag with sandwiches and a thermos flask of tea, in which Mother would have put together that morning.

Once off the lorry everyone would be given a sack and shown to a row of peas or some other produce, for picking. When one filled the sack it was taken to the farmer who would weigh it on a large set of industrial scales, and then make payment determined by the weight of the sack. As a small boy

45

I was never very good at it, but Mother was very quick and filled the hessian bags speedily.

At that time sweets were very difficult to get, as sugar, which had to be imported, was low on the list of war requirements. On one occasion while we were in the fields Dad arrived with a box of Mars Bars. I had never seen or heard of them before and they were a real treat. He gave me half of one, after which I was very disappointed when the remainder were cut into pieces and shared out.

In its wisdom the War Office turned this farm into an army camp with an Ack-Ack gun facility. Half round corrugated Nissan huts were built for accommodation, after which a regiment of the Royal Artillery moved in, there were also dining rooms, offices and guard rooms with all the paraphernalia which the army brings with it.

Away from the buildings and in the fields where vegetables had been grown before the war, gun emplacements were built surrounded by sand bags, a simple and quick method designed to deflect the blast from exploding bombs, so that the guns could continue to operate and fire at the enemy planes.

The Army to boost morale at a time when there was nothing happening war wise and to keep the men happy who were in most cases many miles from home and loved ones, they would hold parties in the camp's canteen inviting local people to mix with men who served there. Soldiers that could play a musical instrument would form a band and while the parents partied and danced we children were confined to a small room, because we were not allowed in the area where alcohol was being served as it was totally illegal.

A little bit further away another large area had been taken over and converted to an airfield which was to become the very famous Fairlop Aerodrome, a fighter plane station where

Spitfires and Hurricanes were based; it was one of the many airfields they flew from in the Battle of Britain.

Not too far away in Dagenham were the vast docks where imports and exports went through. There were also different factories making various items all dedicated to the war effort. Fords motor plant built everything from engines to complete cars and lorries. The large Dagenite Batteries plant which manufactured vehicle electrics. Beckton Gas works producing gas from coal to supply the factories and households. A little nearer to home was the Goodmayes Railway Marshalling Yards in East London. This was one of the largest in England at that time, where rail trucks carrying war material were shunted into the right order behind a rail engine, to be taken to their destination which was marked on their side and could be anywhere around the country.

To explain how this was done the rail line went over a hump, the other side of which were points in the track to direct the wagon into the correct column. The engine would push the truck up the slope of the hump, the engine then backed off to get the next wagon; the one on the hump would roll down the other side and under its own momentum travel down to join the correct line. When it got there, it hit the end wagon with a large bang which could be heard over a considerable area. The reason for telling these events is because we lived about two miles away and we could hear, on most nights, the bangs. I think in today's environment the public would complain bitterly, but it was accepted as part of life and one lived with it and after a time got used to it and was not noticed.

A little further along the River Thames going towards London were the Royal Group of Docks, Royal Albert – Royal Victoria – King George V all named after members of the royal family, not owned by them. This area of water was vast, and still is, making them the largest enclosed docks in the world with an area of 250 acres (1 km$^{2)}$. Including the land facilities, for loading and unloading ships which makes it four times larger. As a matter of interest, building started in 1880 and finished in 1921. All these facilities the enemy would want to destroy and they were all within a few miles from our house. Not that it occurred to me at the time but it must have been something that my parents thought about.

Something else that did not occur to me was the speed that the aerodrome and the Army camp were built. This must have been very impressive by today's standards considering there were no computers, hence detailed drawings would have been processed by hand. Before the war there were not too many mechanical diggers, a lot of the work would have been with shovels and wheel barrows. Quite an achievement and very different to how things are designed and built today.

Fairlop, with its long flat tarmac runways and other facilities was left unchanged when the RAF moved out a little after the war ended in 1945. The aerodrome became a wonderful playground for us lads, we would cycle down the lanes to get to the deserted runways, taking picnics and spend the day having cycle races or some other type of adventure. The place was huge with all types of bunkers, buildings and grassed areas that had been left; the perfect place to make up all types of games with friends.

**

I was about ten years old when father insisted that I should go to Sunday school at the Anglican Church just off Chadwell Heath High Road. I do not know why it suddenly became an issue. My thoughts are now that perhaps Mother wanted me to be brought up as a Catholic. The teaching for the school was held in a timber built hall to the rear of the Church and held in mid-afternoon. From there it was a small step to singing in the choir for the church services held on Sunday mornings and evenings. I must confess that I found it all very boring but I must have looked cute, although uncomfortable, in a black cassock with a white smock over. Singing in the choir twice and going to the wooden hut in the afternoon did mean there was not a lot left of Sundays.

It was the same church where fifteen years later Jean and I would get married and the Reverend Marshall was still in attendance.

# The War

*This picture taken after a night raid appears a bit strange with the milkman, but no doubt he is delivering milk to a WVS (Woman's Voluntary Service) mobile canteen which would have been set up to give refreshments to the firemen and other workers looking for survivors. They can be seen in the background near the smoke caused by the explosion. (Picture from Wikipedia)*

If I may I would like to take the reader back to 1855, for no other reason than being born before the Second World War, we

Londoners were very proud of our heritage, in those days it was the capital of the world, well at least the British Empire, which some people today would say 'That was not to be proud of.'

In 1855 an Act of Parliament was passed to allow the building of the first part of the London Underground Railway system, work on which started a short time later and after a grand opening the first trains started running in 1863, and became the first underground railway in the world.

*Construction of the Metropolitan line in the north of London at King's Cross in 1861 (Picture from Wikipedia)*

The first trains were pulled by steam locomotives but like the system itself, which evolved and grew larger so did the locomotives pulling the carriages when they were replaced with electric driven ones in 1890.

Another interesting thing is the way it was constructed by pulling down buildings, called *the cut and cover method.* This included people's homes, although as Solicitor Pearson, who was a driving force at the time in the argument for the system, said 'most are just slums and need replacing'. Once the ground was levelled a trench was dug, the rail lines laid and then the hole was covered over.

The expansion of the underground continued and from being the largest in the world it now ranks at third with its 270 stations and 250 miles of track, 48% of which is underground.

In the 1930s it was still being extended when the Central Line of the system was being expanded out to Hainault in Essex. By now the cut and cover method of construction had been replaced by a tunnelling procedure. At the start of the war in 1939, the tunnels and the stations on this expansion were complete in the sense of building work but there were no rail lines or plant in place.

The Plessey Company, which made radio parts and other electronic systems, had a modern factory on the Eastern Avenue, not far from the East Road junction. To protect the work they were doing for the war effort, a lot of their manufacturing was moved to the tunnels of the incomplete rail network, where they would be safe from enemy bombing.

*The picture above is of people sheltering in an underground railway station, making themselves comfortable for the night where the rail tracks will eventually be laid. When the trains finally start to run, which will be sometime after the war, they will stop at the platform which is shown on the right of the picture. In the distance, also on the right, the circular entrance to the tunnels can be seen with a row of lights in it. (The picture is taken from Wikipedia.)*

The semi-completed station at Redbridge near Wanstead in east London was part of the new unfinished line and became an air raid shelter. People would go down the many steps − as the lifts were not yet working, with blankets, pillows and food for supper − to spend the night away from the risk of being caught out when the German planes were overhead.

In the early 1940s the country was in fearful limbo waiting for the air raids to start which Germany had used on other cities across Europe. But for the odd warning of an attack nothing transpired, although everyone was expecting on a daily basis for the bombers to arrive and were taking precautions.

I remember before the shelter in our garden was built we went to Redbridge Station on a number of nights, but it was a long way from where we lived, about three miles along the Eastern Avenue. On one occasion after a night trying to sleep in the cold of the tunnel on the hard ground while some men were making a fair amount of noise playing cards, and I think Dad was amongst them. We made our way up the steps of the proposed station. When we arrived in the open we were told there had been an air attack overnight which had resulted in no buses running. There was no choice and we had to walk the three miles or so home. Carrying the blankets and other items we had taken to make the night as comfortable as possible. I do not think we went again after that.

In the front room at East Road there was a long tall heavy sideboard, made of hard wood, against one wall, with mirrors along the top and an opening below about two feet square along its length. In front of it and taking up most of the middle of the room was a big, rectangular, heavy, wooden table. Instead of the long trip to Redbridge, beds were made under the furniture as protection if the worst should happen.

At this time the Anderson Shelter was still being made ready, thick concrete had been formed around the base of the internal walls to give it extra support, but the floor was left in its original earthen state, also bunk beds were being constructed to make the best use of the confined space.

The summer of 1940 crept past with the odd air raid otherwise there was little activity from the skies. It was known that the Germans were preparing landing barges on the east coast of France for an invasion across the English Channel. In the cinemas the Pathè News showed pictures of these landing barges lined up adjacent to the French Ports. This brought a new fear to the people.

Although very little was happening war wise there were many shortages, sweets had vanished from the shelves and by the spring of 1940 most food was rationed. There were some exceptions as some food which was produced locally was not normally included in the rationing regulations, but those items were in short supply and very rarely obtainable.

In that period twenty million tons of food a year was being imported into England to feed a population of forty-six million people. The German forces targeted the ships heading for the UK, and in the early part of the conflict were doing a lot of damage to our supply routes.

To help overcome the losses the 'U' Boats were causing, the Ministry of food issued every person with a *Ration Book* limiting the amount of food one could buy. To obtain one of these, the populace had to register at one shop to obtain their supplies. The ministry would provide the shop with enough food for those people registered with it. The ration book itself contained coupons which could only be used on the date marked on it, which controlled the amount of provisions required in the system.

Most bread at that time was baked by small local bakers. To help in stopping wastage the Ministry decreed bread could only be sold a day old, the reasoning being new uncut bread, that is how a loaf was normally made, was too fresh to cut thinly and when fresh it was too tasty and people would eat too much.

Preparations for the war were being made whilst waiting for the enemy to make a move, otherwise people went about their business as best they could, always carrying their gas masks. The government posted signs throughout the country trying to restrict travel to only what was necessary and to dig for victory by growing your own food.

In the early part of the war Dad had been called up into the Army. I remember quite clearly the day he went away − I was sitting at the big table in the front room when he asked me if I would miss him. I did not understand what he meant and stuttered before replying 'No' at which he and Mother laughed and said I should have answered 'Yes'.

Historians looking back at this period are convinced that if Hitler had used this time to attack the UK, Germany could have won. Instead the government was given months of grace which allowed our defences and armed forces to become stronger.

This all changed on $6^{th}$ September 1940. There had not been an air raid for a long time and we had got used to staying in the house in the evening. We were sitting at home when the air raid warning sounded. At first, not a lot of notice was taken; there had been a lot of trial runs and testing of the systems before that night. It had been quiet for so long we did not know that this was the start of Hitler's determination to bring Great Britain to its knees.

When the guns started firing from the Army camp we knew it was for real. We could hear the gunfire from the *Ack-Ack* guns which indicated the enemy planes were not very far away. There was not a lot of time as we could hear bombs being dropped so with Mother and baby Bob, I squeezed in the cupboard under the stairs; many weeks before that, Mum had cleared the bedding from under the sideboard convinced that no planes were ever coming. Dad and Frances, my sister, were under the big, solid wooden table in the front room.

At first I think we all thought it would be over very quickly and although we were uncomfortable it was bearable, but it was not to be. It was a long time in that cramped space waiting for the noise to stop and the all clear to sound. Even today, as I write this, we were recently watching a feature on the television about the blitz of 70 years previously. In the programme there was the sound of an air raid warning, my heart did a little flutter and I had a brief moment of fear.

The following early evening it was quiet and we were preparing for bed, when a lot later than the previous day, the sirens started their wailing and the guns were firing once more. We left the comfort of the house in our night clothes to go to the air raid shelter in the middle of the garden. After the stay in the cupboard of the evening before, a lot of effort had gone in to get it finished during the day so that we could sleep there.

The total floor area of the interior of the Anderson was not much larger than a normal size double bed, and the floor was about a metre below ground level. Even as a five-year-old I had to duck my head to get in the entrance. When we first arrived, it was dry and there was a small, round oil stove with a blue flame on the floor to give some heat. But oil stoves give off moisture which did not help with the condensation problem.

On both sides of the shelter, narrow wooden bunk beds had been constructed against the walls. *Beds* is a poor word for them as they did not have any form of springs, just a wood covering beneath a very thin mattress. On each side there was one on the ground with another above, and a small one going across the rear wall for baby Bob to sleep in.

There were no windows, only the small opening for the door, which had a blast protecting wall of sand bags on the outside in case a bomb fell nearby. The theory was the wall would redirect the blast away from the shelter. The internal walls were smooth, galvanised corrugated iron curving over into an arch with no through ventilation. With five people breathing plus the oil stove − the cold walls and the roof soon became soaking wet with condensation, the water running down in rivulets onto the blankets and bedding.

*The picture is of an Anderson shelter being built. (From Wikipedia)*

There was no door on the entrance way which allowed some air to enter the confined space, but it was freezing air especially in the winter months. Not very comfortable for sleeping, it was extremely damp and cold and another problem was when it rained the floor would get very wet.

It was exceedingly traumatic for us children. There was no set routine. During the day going to school on your own, and it did not matter if it was raining or even snowing, you still went, looking up into the sky as you did so to see if any planes were lurking around. Sometimes it was possible to hear gunfire or bombs dropping in the distance.

At first the feeling was that the bombing and the nightly raids would soon stop, but they didn't. For a five-year-old a night is a long time, a week a lot longer but a month is an age. But imagine the raids becoming a nightly occurrence, going on for month after month, lack of sleep, the constant fear of wondering when and where the next explosion would be. The sheer terror – not only in the nights but to hear a plane during the day would set your heart beating.

The German aircraft very rarely called during the daylight hours, but occasionally the warnings would sound and then if you were out and about, it was a matter of running to the nearest shelter. These had been built by the authorities, normally tall, (*well I was only small*) brick structures with flat concrete roofs on the side of streets. Once inside, you stood with others who had been caught in the open and waited for the all clear, and that could be a very long time.

There was a report of an air raid shelter in central London which could hold 400 people and of a similar construction as described above. This shelter, because of its size, had a ventilation shaft a few feet in diameter going out through the roof. By sheer bad luck a German bomb entered the shaft and exploded in the shelter killing the people inside. Shelters did protect against the blast of these terrible weapons but we were all aware in the event of a direct hit they were little protection. In Dagenham a few of the shelters were hit with a bomb, all that remained afterwards was a large crater, some remains of the shelter scattered around but no sign of the occupants. *(See William Riddiford in Google search.)*

Another item which was common to see on the side of the road was large black steel water tanks twenty to thirty feet in length and probably about six feet wide. Beside them fixed to brackets were stirrup pumps, these were similar to bicycle pumps, with a hose which was put in the tank and another to point at a fire in the hope of putting it out. These tanks were about five to six feet tall and on hot days we would climb into them for a swim. The authorities stopped this pleasure by putting wire netting across the top.

There were also lines of large concrete square blocks which would stretch in rows in areas where it was deemed, if the enemy landed on our shores and advanced inland, then it was hoped these large blocks would slow the movement of their tanks. Beside the concrete structures were large steel angle irons to fill the gaps between them so as to block the roads if the need arose.

One of the saddest sights of that time was after an air raid to see a house that had taken a direct hit which would just be a pile of rubble. The properties to each side would also be damaged and it was not uncommon for a side wall to have been destroyed leaving rooms complete with furniture suspended in the open on a sloping unsupported floor, small personal items scattered about.

When Father had been *'called up'* for war service in the Army, Mother did not expect to see him until the conflict ended. But he had always suffered with stomach problems and was discharged from the forces as being unfit. How or why he started working on the docks I do not know but no doubt as an electrician he would have been ordered to carry out work in the London Docks helping in the repair of war damaged ships. It was about five or six mile cycle ride, maybe more which he would do twice a day, and on arriving home after a brief meal he would be ready to attend the local Home Guard Centre for duty. He would stay out at night, with others as a look out for unexploded or fire bombs which were being dropped, also to be of assistance if anything happened.

Every night was the same, we would put coats on over our night wear and make our way down the garden and huddle together in what was to become known as *The Dug Out*. The air raids would start after dark and go on for hours as we lay on the bunks listening to the ceaseless drone of the bombers overhead, hearing the bombs whistling out of the sky, wondering each time where they were heading.

Some explosions were just a crump in the distance, other times a lot nearer, the noise so loud, the ground and the shelter violently shaking, we would be convinced our house had been hit. Sleep was not possible, sometimes just dozing when there was a lull in the war that was raging outside, all the time feeling very cold.

In the years leading up to the war with Britain, the Germans had used a method known as Blitzkrieg (*lightning war*) to invade other countries. When Hitler had made a decision with his Generals of the nation they wanted to invade and conquer, they would put a well-established and successful invasion technique in place. Their method was to send hundreds of bombers to drop heavy bombs on the countries cities and defences to bring the people into submission, so that when their ground forces followed this bombardment there was very little fight left in the country they had invaded.

With the horror their powerful forces could inflict from the air, which they used to demoralise the populous before the start of their attack, most of Europe had no answer and were quickly overrun by Hitler's troops. It was now our turn, starting with the air raids.

*"The Battle of France is over, I expect the Battle of*
*Britain is about to begin"*
*Sir Winston Churchill 1940.*

The nearby Army camp with its *Ack Ack* fire power had various other guns. Beside the loud noise of the standard guns there was one we nick-named *Big Berther*, when it fired, there was a loud bang and the ground seemed to shake, what it was used for we never knew.

In between times, the *Pom Poms* would be going off in fast sequence. It was a gun that could fire shells in quick succession, some of which would be tracers. A tracer is like the lighted tail of a rocket firework going high into the air showing the gunners where their aim was. The search lights would be piercing the night sky looking for the enemy, when one was found, the tracers would search it out so that the shells following would make a hit.

Through all this we lay in the shelter very quietly, no one saying a word, just listening to the thundering noise, hoping Dad was alright, wondering and wishing it would soon stop. But the months were to roll by and the German planes were intent on doing as much damage as they could. For 176 consecutive nights, I have since read; they continued their bombardment night after night.

*Bombed houses in London 1940 (From Wikipedia)*

Each morning after the beautiful sound of the single note of the siren giving the 'all clear', we would leave the safety of the Anderson shelter. The enemy rarely came during the daylight hours. Scattered around the garden and in the streets would be pieces of shrapnel that had dropped out of the sky, the remains of the shells that had been fired from our guns, sometimes a piece of aircraft among them.

*Children in the East End of London, made homeless by the random bombs of the Nazi night raiders, outside the wreckage of what was their "home". September 1940*
*(From Wikipedia)*

As winter approached, the war rumbled on in all its intensity. The sky every night lit by the tracers from the *Pom Poms*, search lights weaving across the dark sky, white smoke caught in their light as the *Ack Ack* shells exploded high in the air. The flashes from the exploding shells lighting up the sky, also the silver coloured Barrage Balloons swinging on their steel cables, tethered at a few hundred feet to stop low flying enemy aircraft from strafing the ground.

Above it all was the sound and the drone of engines from the bombers, their bombs screaming down, with explosions and gun fire from the local Army camp. Sometimes it was possible to be able to distinguish the lighter sound of the fighter planes as they swooped in the sky searching out their prey. Amongst all this, the bombers would drop flares on parachutes to light up the ground so they could see the targets they wanted to aim at.

*The picture is of Coventry City Centre following a raid on 16th Nov 1940 (from Wikipedia)*

As the months drifted by, the enemy were not letting up. Each night the sirens would wail as another raid started. On one occasion they bombed the Beckton Gas works. The result of which there was no gas in the house to cook with. So meals were heated over the open fire, even this was a problem as coal was in short supply and people would look for and sort out different types of fuel to keep the fire alight for meal times and to keep warm.

There was no fixed pattern; sometimes just as it got dark there would be an air raid warning. Other times, when the family were convinced the enemy were not coming, sitting warm around the fire or getting ready to go to bed, the familiar sound of the air raid warning would be heard. We would look at each other and it was off to the cold, damp, musty shelter.

The raids also varied in intensity, some nights the action was in the distance, nearer the city of London where further Docks were. Other nights the Luftwaffe (*German Air Force*), would concentrate their efforts closer to our home, the airfield at Fairlop, the factories and docks in Dagenham, and a little nearer to home the railway marshalling yards at Goodmayes. When these places were their targets, the noise would be deafening with the smell of cordite and burning in the air.

On the odd occasion during the evening, Dad wearing his Army issue tin hat, would look in through the small opening to the shelter, exchanging a few words of comfort with Mother. One evening when the raid was particularly harsh, he came rushing to the dugout. With no time for an explanation he insisted Mum follow him, we lay there fearfully, wondering what was happening.

After a while Mum returned and explained, a German airman whose plane had been shot down, had drifted down and landed in the street a few doors down from our house. The panic was to share the silk from the parachute. The risk of bombs and shrapnel falling, all being ignored as our neighbours shared out the material amongst themselves. Where the plane crashed or of its remains I do not know, nor what happened to the airman.

I also do not remember what happened to the silk material of the parachute or if it was of any use to the new owners. The excitement in the street was because any form of cloth was in short supply, and could only be bought if your coupon ration was adequate. Something dropping out of the sky was not to be scoffed at. What I do remember is Mum was very good on a sewing machine and maybe she made something out of it.

It was many months later that the Germans, after receiving constant heavy losses from our fighter planes and defences, gave up, but not before they had destroyed a third of the housing stock in London. *(That is one house in three.)* Other cities also suffered equally as badly from the damage done by the bombing. By then we had spent a long time in the cold and sometimes wet sleepless nights in the Anderson shelter.

It was May 1941 when the Germans finally gave up the struggle to bring Britain to its knees, the night time raids were not so frequent although the war continued elsewhere. Hitler had turned his attention and most of his forces to Russia in the east of Europe.

After a few nights of silence we returned to our beds in the house. However, the nightmares did not go away, there was always the fear of the dark and imaginations of what was under the bed, so we would run and jump on it in case something, or an escaped German, was hiding underneath and may grab your feet as you got in.

It was later that year in December 1941 when the Japanese joined the war, although before that date, and since 1937, they had been at war with China. In that month on the seventh, a few weeks before Christmas, they launched a surprise air attack on Pearl Harbour: a United States naval station in the Pacific. This action brought the USA into the war.

I would just like to add, over the years, a lot has been said about the damage the allies caused to German cities during the bombing that was inflicted later in the war by British and American air forces, especially to Dresden – I would agree, in as much it should not have been. But on the other hand, how do you fight a dictator, who had since the nineteen thirties, destroyed many cities − not only ours but others, and had murdered hundreds of thousands if not millions of people? On an earlier page is a picture of what he achieved in one night in Coventry. The German forces having done that sort of damage, as in that image, too many towns and cities across Europe. And also in the one hundred and seventy-six continuous nights they destroyed the third of the housing stock in London. Did he really believe he was not vulnerable to similar reprisals?

\*\*

In the early 1940s I started attending the Warren Secondary Modern School, which was in Whalebone Lane, which was for boys only. Girls had another section to the rear of the property, which was strictly out of bounds to us lads

As stated earlier, Whalebone Lane was part of the main route to the docks, which are on the banks of the deep waters of the river Thames, along with the Ford Motor company. Frequently we would see, from the school playground, convoys of military vehicles going south, sometimes rows of Jeeps other times lines of lorries or amphibious DUKW all going towards Dagenham, and no doubt the facilities offered there.

It was one sunny afternoon when walking home from school, when I heard an engine noise of a plane, and then gun fire; it was a little way away. This continued for some time, probably less than a minute but it seemed longer. The people out in the open were lucky if they did not get hit as there had been no air raid warning for them to take shelter.

I learned later that it had been a German Messerschmitt, a fighter plane, which had flown low over Chadwell Heath High Road, strafing the road with its machine guns, making two passes causing casualties and damage. The last time I was in Chadwell Heath, about forty years after the end of the war, some of the bullet marks were still there on the side of the buildings that had survived the years.

Who would do such a thing, mowing down women and children as they went about their daily lives? Children being collected from the nearby junior school, while others mothers/grandmothers as they shopped in the many retail premises to be found in the High Street. Did the pilot think it was a game shooting up an area with no military involvement, or was he instructed to carry out the action from a higher authority?

One of the worst problems that the home front had during the period of the German bombing was the shortage of resources and man power to deal with the damage as it was happening. The Palace of Westminster, (*House of Commons*) was bombed fourteen times during the blitz. During the night of 10/11th May 1941 the bombers were back again and many incendiaries landed on the roof of the building. The fire-fighters were outnumbered and there was not enough equipment to pump water to cope with the flames. Their choice was either to try and save the Common's Chamber where Members of Parliament debated or the more ancient Westminster Hall. They went for the latter. The Chamber was destroyed and finally rebuilt but not completed until 1952.

St Paul's Cathedral in London was hit many times throughout the blitz and the many months of continuous bombing, the volunteers posted on the roof did a valiant job of dowsing the many incendiary bombs that were dropped on the building.

*This picture is of the famous St Paul's Cathedral, London, after an air raid. The picture was taken by Herbert Mason on 29th December 1940 from the Daily Mail building and was published two days later.*

It has often been said that it is a wonder a lot of churches survived as if they were being looked after by a power above, it could also be said about other land marks like Tower Bridge in London. But I have a different theory I think they survived because the bombers used them as markers to identify other more important targets; without radar in their planes, these tall buildings in cities and towns would confirm their location and no doubt lead them to their proposed destination.

By this time the tide of war was turning and everyday there would be flights of Allied Bombers darkening the skies as they made their way on bombing missions against the enemy. The familiar drone coming from the planes of our Air Force was comforting and so very different to the noise of the German ones. We would stare skywards counting the craft as they flew past. They would go out in strict formation. It would be hours later when we would watch the survivors struggling back in ones and twos as they made their way home, some with smoke gently pouring into their slip streams.

*St Katherine's Docks in East London after a night time raid in 1940*

*Addendum I*

Talking to Bob recently, a friend of many years, he told me the story of when he was at school. The first job in the morning on arrival was to go around the playground and collect the shrapnel that had fallen the night before. Arriving one day, amongst the sharp pieces of metal lying on the ground was an open box with sticks in it so he took one, as a keepsake.

He proudly took it home and placed it on the mantel piece. His mother arrived and had a small fit when she saw it; she promptly put it into a bag and insisted he take it to the Police Station. With some pride when he arrived there, he put it on the desk explaining that he had found it; the man in charge cleared the premises and called the bomb squad. The sticks were incendiaries that had not ignited.

Bob also tells the story of living in a terraced house in South London. Opposite was a Fish & Chip shop, a bomb fell demolishing the shop whilst he was at home with his mother. Their house took the full blast from the explosion and collapsed. The two of them had to be rescued and were pulled out of the rubble covered in dust. There are a million other stories just like it, but not all with a good ending of a rescue, so many were fatal.

*Addendum II*

In every town there were Civil Defence Wardens, each working shifts to be available in the event of air attack, they would help with clearing the debris and looking after the injured, after an assault. The picture on the following page is one of the many East London Crews, this group from Ilford in 1940.

At the time there was a severe shortage of purpose built ambulances and there was a need for more vehicles to help with the injured from the air raids, so civil vans and cars were used. The ambulance in the picture is nothing more than an elderly van called into serve and probably had no more than stretchers with perhaps a medical kit in the rear of it. Because of the strict black out laws any form of light showing during the hours of darkness was forbidden. The man on the left who is leaning over the car headlight, note the cowling over the front of the light unit to prevent aircraft from seeing the vehicle at night, it also meant the driver could not see a great deal either. The other head light has a hood over it and the lens has been blanked out with a number on it, the wording says 'A CAR' which no doubt glowed at night and had some meaning to other rescuers.

### *Addendum III*

William Riddiford, the father of Eve, my brother-in-law's partner, was an ARP *(Air Raid Precautions)* during the war and wrote a diary of the events of the period. These diaries have recently been published by Barking and Dagenham Council. The wording is Williams and no doubt written at a difficult time. What follows is a sample taken from his work which goes to 70 pages; the completed set can be seen on Google (type in William Riddiford in the search square). As I've said the wording is Williams as he wrote it during that terrible period.

### Saturday 7 September 1940
Take Cover warning 12.00am – 1.10am

Off Duty. Heavy bombs heard Barking direction. Elsie, Evelyn and Mother slept in Shelter all night

Take Cover warning 5.00pm – 6.45pm

On Duty. The Largest Raid yet. Three relays. came straight up the Thames, turned at Woolwich, West Ham, Ilford, and Hainault direction, terrible fires made each side of the river, great fire Becton direction, the River Thames one mass of black smoke, from Becton and Woolwich down to Tilbury as far as we could see. We counted dozen of enemy planes:

350 planes took part; 88 brought down.

### Friday 20 September 1940
Take Cover warning 11.00am – 12.00am

Take Cover warning 8.30pm – 5.00am

On Duty. The longest and 8½ hours most heaviest night raid yet. Very heavy gun fire nearly all night. The great Woolwich and Becton fire lit the whole sky; no gas on Sunday, people cooking by fires. Dad found 5 pieces of shrapnel on school premises Off Duty. Slight gun fire. Many planes heard. Fairly quiet here.

Take Cover warning 7.55pm – 12.30am

Off Duty. Dad and myself just heard 5 minutes of the 9 o'clock news, then we rushed back in the shelter because of heavy firing overhead when there was several terrific bangs and bits of stone and dirt was falling on the garden and on the greenhouse. We were frightened to come out for a few minutes because of delayed action bombs, then we heard a lot of shouting in the road. We came out and the path and road was smothered with dirt and stones. A bomb had dropped about 80 yards away in a back garden, near a shelter, no one hurt. Another about 45 yards, in the road, in front of the big gates of the school playground shattered the roof of the black house, damaged Barritt's shop roof, big crater in the road, flung kerb stones over the house and into the playground, no one hurt. Another in Bonham Gardens in between 4 shelters. 22 people in the 4 shelters, one boy slight head injury, about 130 yards. Another about 150 yards Valence Wood Road. Delayed action, several houses evacuated, had not gone off by Sunday 22nd.

Another 150 yards Warrington Road smashed 3 houses down to the ground, no one hurt, people in their shelters. Another about 400 yards Lymington School playground. Another about 500 yards Barton's Bakeries, 12 hurt.

### BBC News Broadcast September 1940:
*Repeated from the first pages of this book*

**London blitzed by German bombers** The German air force has unleashed a wave of heavy bombing raids on London, killing hundreds of civilians and injuring many more. The Ministry of Home Security said the scale of the attacks was the largest the Germans had yet attempted. "Our defences have actively engaged the enemy at all points," said a communiqué issued this evening. "The civil defence services are responding admirably to all calls that are being made upon them."

The first raids came towards the end of the afternoon, and were concentrated on the densely populated East End, along the river by London's docks. About 300 bombers attacked the city for over an hour and a half. The entire docklands area seemed to be ablaze as hundreds of fires lit up the sky. Once darkness fell, the fires could be seen more than 10 miles away, and it is believed that the light guided a second wave of German bombers which began coming over at about 2030 BST (1930 GMT).

The night bombing lasted over eight hours, shaking the city with the deafening noise of hundreds of bombs falling so close together there was hardly a pause between them.

One bomb exploded on a crowded air raid shelter in an East London district.

In what was described as "a million to one chance", the bomb fell directly on the 3ft (90cm) by 1ft (30cm) ventilation shaft − the only vulnerable place in a strongly-protected underground shelter which could accommodate over 1,000 people.

About 14 people are believed to have been killed and 40 injured, including children.

Civil defence workers worked through the night, often in the face of heavy bombing, to take people out of the range of fire and find them temporary shelter and food.

An official paid tribute to staff at one London hospital which was hit, saying, "They showed marvellous bravery, keeping on until bomb detonations and gunfire made it absolutely impossible."

In the air, a series of ferocious dogfights developed as the German aircraft flew up the Thames Estuary.

The Air Ministry says at least 15 enemy aircraft crashed into the estuary, and in all, the Ministry said, 88 German aircraft were shot down, against 22 RAF planes lost.

### The Blitz (From Wikipedia)

*The Blitz was the sustained bombing of Britain by Nazi Germany between 6 September 1940 and 10 May 1941, during the Second World War. The Blitz hit many towns and cities across the country, but it began with the bombing of London for 76 consecutive nights. By the end of May 1941, over 43,000 civilians, half of them in London, had been killed by bombing and more than a million houses were destroyed or damaged in London alone.*

*London was not the only city to suffer Luftwaffe bombing during the Blitz. Other important military and industrial centres, such as Aberdeen, Barrow-in-Furness, Belfast, Bootle, Birkenhead, Wallasey, Birmingham, Bristol, Cardiff, Clydebank, Coventry, Exeter, Glasgow, Greenock, Sheffield, Swansea, Liverpool, Kingston upon Hull, Manchester,*

_Portsmouth,_ _Plymouth,_ _Nottingham,_ _Brighton,_ _Eastbourne,_ _Sunderland,_ and _Southampton,_ suffered heavy air raids and high numbers of casualties. Hull was the most heavily bombed city after London with 85% of its buildings being destroyed or affected. _Birmingham_ and _Coventry_ were very badly affected because of the Spitfire and Tank plant being based in Birmingham and the many other munitions factories in Coventry. Coventry was almost totally destroyed.

Smaller bombing raids were made on _Edinburgh,_ _Newcastle,_ _York,_ _Exeter,_ and _Bath._ Oxford was spared; Bodleian Library spokesman Oana Romocea said: "It's thought Hitler was never intent on bombing Oxford because he wanted to make it the new capital of his new kingdom." _Blackpool_ was hit by only 45 high explosive bombs. One theory put forward is that Hitler was saving Blackpool as a recreation centre for his troops after he had taken England. A more likely suggestion is that Blackpool having three piers sticking into the sea, acted as a marker for aircraft heading for Manchester, Liverpool or the shipyard at Barrow. Hitler's aim was to destroy British civilian and government morale.

# A New Horror

A warm sunny day with its shadows lying across the ground, the soft wind rustling in the leaves of the trees, birds singing in the nearby hedgerows. Amongst this tranquillity the bowler paced out his run. Turning, he took a few quick steps and the cricket ball left his hand and whistled through the air, the cricketer lifts his bat ready to respond, swinging it making a solid hit, sending the ball to the boundary.

The boundary was the fence on the other side of The Close, a little turning off East Road. The fielders moved quickly to recover the ball as the batsman made a quick run to the other tree that lined the small turning, opposite the one that was used as a wicket. The ball was not really a cricket ball but an old tennis ball and the bat a shaped piece of wood, to suit the occasion.

In the summer, when everyone was talking about cricket scores or the results of some other game, we would make that sport the current pastime. There were no personalities back then, one side would be Australia the other England or maybe two football teams, whatever the current game was in the news.

As the seasons changed so did the professional games. Then the tree would become a goal post or maybe the home run for a game of rounders. It only needed imagination to change its function. Sometimes it was the finishing post for a race of self-built go-carts, (wheel barrows) made from pieces of wood and some old wheels normally from an old upright pram, with a length of string to steer the front ones which had been modified normally with a plank of wood with a nut and bolt to the centre so they would steer. If you were unlucky then you did the pushing.

If the machine you had spent many hours building, had no brakes then who cared? Putting your shoed foot on the front wheels had the same effect! Even greater fun if a wheel should come off and the driver fell out. It didn't really matter if you grazed your knee, hand or whatever; you got up, brushed the offending part and started again.

I find it a little sad when I now see toddlers or children riding on factory built plastic toys, nowhere near the fun or education of building your own.

When we got bored with the carts or playing games around the tree then we would go for a cycle ride, but first you had to have a bike. There was no money to buy one, and anyway, because of the war they were not being made for home use as metal was required elsewhere. But somehow we found them or bits of bikes which people had in their garden sheds and would happily part with the item. We lads would be busy gathering the pieces including spanners and screw drivers to build a cycle that could be ridden. A frame from somewhere – then a wheel and a chain – somebody would have a spare pair of handlebars and eventually one would have enough parts to make up a complete machine.

Schooling during the war was a sort of hit-and-miss affair. Good, young, progressive teachers had been transferred to the armed forces, to do their part in the war effort. The authorities had to look elsewhere, and one of the answers was to bring back teachers who had retired. To our young eyes they looked really ancient. One thing was for certain, come rain, sun or snow, no matter how deep, school would be open and that is where you went.

Lessons did not follow a set formula, as teachers changed frequently. A maths lesson under one person could be learning the time tables; $2 \times 2 = 4$, $2 \times 3 = 6$, $2 \times 4 = 8$ and so on, perhaps repeating the full spectrum for the hour's lesson.

When it was time to have the subject again, then another teacher would appear and maybe start teaching algebra, not at the start of basics but somewhere in the middle of a normal term lesson. All of which I, and I am sure others, found very confusing, not understanding the meaning of it at all. Sometimes just when you got into understanding what was being taught then it would be somebody else's turn to part with knowledge to a class of boys who were worried because of the war, or depressed because they had lost family or friends.

On another day, perhaps there would be no one who could teach the subject, so one of the staff would take us out into the playground to play hockey. In fact I became very good at hockey. Instead of hockey perhaps the instructor was used to teaching art so the lesson would change completely and we would spend the time painting or drawing.

While the school was trying hard to give us an education it would sometimes be interrupted by an air raid warning. I have tried to remember where the shelters were at the school, I can remember lining up to go to them, I cannot say accurately where, although I think they were built of red brick in the playground. Perhaps because of the sheer terror of it, time has blanked it out.

The Warren Boys' Comprehensive School was to the east side of Whalebone Lane, with the playground to one side on the right. To the rear of the single-story building was the girls' section and beyond that farmed vegetable fields that sloped down to the town of Romford, which could be seen in the distance about three miles away.

One day we were playing outside during the break, when a shout went up, one of the lads had spotted a dog fight with fighter planes over Romford.

The playground extended down past the girls' school, whose playtime was immediately after the boys. We were not allowed into the area where the females took their break, but I and a few others rushed down to look at what was going on. One of Germany's new horrors a V1 bomb, a Doodlebug, as shown above, was flying over Romford heading for the fields and our school. These things flew in a straight line and were pilotless; the noise they made was a continuous drone.

There were two Spitfires chasing and swooping on to it, their guns firing in quick succession trying to shoot it down, or they would try and flip the bomb over by tipping one of its wings using their own wing to do it. My guess was so it would crash into the fields where it could only damage crops. They were not successful as suddenly the engine stopped and the Bug started to glide out of the sky.

We watched its descent and somewhere over to the left a mile or so away, a puff of smoke appeared, rising up from some buildings the sound of the explosion following a few seconds later. It was then we got shouted at by a member of staff for not only being in the girls' playground but for not taking shelter.

By now, after more than four years, the war had taken its toll, with daily reports of people being injured or killed. It had become common place with little time for mourning, especially if you also had to find somewhere to live. On a number of occasions children had come into class crying after losing a loved one or sometimes they did not come at all, because they themselves had become victims.

On one occasion Dennis, who was a friend and sat next to me in class, was crying and full of tears all day, because his Father, a postman, had been killed that morning whilst delivering letters, when a doodlebug had hit the road where he was walking. All very sad but with no meaning to an onlooker – it was a long war, everywhere there were bombed out buildings and many a story of people being dead or injured. Somehow it started to have little significance.

In 1944 it was my brother's turn to go to Japan Road Infants School. *By now, Japan was in the war and it became even more baffling why it was called Japan Road.* The hall in the centre of the primary school, with the large fireplace which I mentioned earlier, had a high ceiling and was part of the roof and in it a glass dome to let daylight in. Whilst my brother was having a lesson below this lighted area a V1's engine had stopped, there was a crash as it glided to earth. It had hit the glass of the sky light, showering the children below with splinters but luckily it did not explode, it continued its flight to where it destroyed the houses beside the park. The school was very lucky as no one was hurt.

On another day in the afternoon, we were in class when we heard an explosion, it sounded very near. After a while one of the staff came into the classroom saying that the houses in East Road had been hit by a Doodlebug. "All those living in East Road put your hand up." Those who did were sent home.

I left the school, it was cloudy and overcast which fitted my mood, feeling very lonely, tears running down my cheeks and full of fear, and wondering what I would find when I arrived. When I turned into our turning I could see smoke and dust rising in the air from the far end of the road – our house was not affected. I walked down to where the horror had landed. It had destroyed about four houses, some shops and the local doctor's surgery. The recovery people were still working in the wreckage moving bricks, wooden beams and other material trying to rescue those buried underneath. The adjoining house of the group had lost its side wall − I stared up in shock looking at the upper storey of the building the floor was sloping down because of the loss of its support − the amazing thing the bedroom was still complete with bed, wardrobes and other furniture.

Worse was yet to come in 1944. We were at home when there was an enormous explosion, I think, as I remember it was a Sunday as my parents were there. The ground shook with the house shuddering, again there had been no warning. It was the first of Hitler's new weapons to explode near us.

The V2 Rocket was a violent horror, many more times worse than the doodlebug, for it dropped out of the sky without warning. The power of its explosives was ten times that of a bomb. There was no noise, although some people said they heard a whistle before the explosion, but nowhere near long enough to be able to react and take cover. The bomb on that

Sunday had landed in Chadwell Heath High Road destroying houses and shops.

This nasty weapon was the first type of rocket to go into space before descending on an unsuspecting public. It was the predecessor to the machines that went to the moon in the sixties.

Despite the fact that Germany was losing the war, as they were being overrun by the combined armies after the allied landings in June 1944, they continued to rain this high explosive device on the civilians in Southern England, and other places killing many thousands of people. It was a weapon that could not be accurately aimed at a target, so it was totally indiscriminate where it landed and exploded and what it destroyed and who was killed.

*The picture is the aftermath of a V-2 bomb at <u>Battersea</u> London, 27 January 1945 (from Wikipedia).*

During the latter part of the war, Mother worked on the red trolley buses that ran out of Chadwell Heath, these vehicles were larger than normal buses carrying and seating over seventy people. From the terminus they went to various places. On one particular day Mum, was the conductress in the rear of the bus collecting fares, they were on the way to Aldgate which is just outside the City of London.

The buses followed the main road that runs from Essex, through Romford and the East End of London where it is known as the London Road. One day Mum was very late getting home and when she finally arrived she was very stressed and tired.

It was a frightening story Mother told, she had also been very lucky as she spoke of what happened. As the trolley bus was about halfway through its journey, approaching Forest Gate, where there is a major crossroads with traffic lights. On one corner the local telephone exchange also rows of shops on both sides of the road. Mum was collecting fares on the lower deck when suddenly there was a loud explosion. This large vehicle full of people on its two floors was blown on to its side.

The V2 rocket, again without warning, had demolished the centre of the town. Houses, rows of shops, a few pubs, the skating rink and the telephone exchange all reduced to a pile of rubble. If the bus that Mum was on had been a little further on its journey it too would have been reduced to nothing. This rocket was a wicked weapon to use against civilians, old or young, rich or poor it did not discriminate.

The people of East Road, at the top end where we lived, and the immediate houses around us, were very lucky as we came through it all with a few broken roof tiles from falling shrapnel, but I don't think there were any windows damaged, although I cannot say if other people from the street were hurt or injured elsewhere.

The following further information taken from Wikipedia describing the two German weapons as described above.

*The **Fieseler Fi 103**, better known as the **V-1** 'Buzz Bomb', (German:* Vergeltungswaffe *1, retaliation weapon), also colloquially known in Britain as the 'Doodlebug', was an early 'pulse-jet-powered' example of what would later be called a <u>'cruise missile'</u>. The V-1 was developed at* Peenemünde Airfield *by the* German Luftwaffe *during the <u>Second World War</u>. The first of the so-called* Vergeltungswaffen *series designed for 'terror bombing' of* London, *the V-1 was fired from "ski" launch sites along the French (*Pas-de-Calais*) and* Dutch *coasts. The first V-1 was launched at London on 13 June 1944, one week after (and prompted by) the successful 'Allied landing in Europe'. At its peak, over a hundred V-1s a day were fired at southeast England, 9,521 in total, decreasing in number as sites were overrun until October 1944, when the last V-1 site in range of Britain was overrun by 'Allied' forces. This caused the remaining V-1s to be re-targeted on the port of* Antwerp *and other targets in Belgium, with 2,448 V-1s being launched. The attacks stopped when the last site was overrun on 29 March 1945. In total, the V-1 attacks caused 22,892 casualties (almost entirely civilians).*

*The **V-2 rocket** (German:* Vergeltungswaffe *2, i.e. reprisal weapon 2), technical name A4, was a long-range 'ballistic missile' that was developed at the beginning of the Second World War in Germany, specifically targeted at Belgium and sites in south-eastern England. The rocket was the world's first long-range combat-ballistic missile and first known human 'artefact' to achieve 'sub-orbital spaceflight'._It was the progenitor of all modern rockets, including those used by the United States and Soviet Union space programs, which gained access to the scientists and designs through 'Operation Paperclip' and 'Operation Osoaviakhim'.*

*Over 3,000 V-2s were launched as military rockets by the German 'Wehrmacht' against Allied targets during the war, mostly London and later Antwerp, resulting in the death of an estimated 7,250 military personnel and civilians.*

# School Plus

It was acclaimed as the first since the beginning of the war, a street party in the middle of the thoroughfare in East Road. I had not experienced anything like it before, there was so much activity with all our neighbours bringing out tables and chairs and placing them in the centre of the carriageway. The end of the war V.E. *(Victory in Europe)* day had been announced a little earlier; our street and others were covered in bunting, streamers with Union Flags from poles or draped from windows.

The neighbours had got together and lined the centre of the road with a mixture of tables and chairs of all sizes and types which had come from different houses, with a variety of table cloths and colours. The picture on the previous page is Winston Churchill waving to the crowds in Whitehall, London on the first day of peace.

People were loading the tables with food and drink all homemade and different. Some surprising items had been laid out, it was obvious that the foresighted in the road had been saving rations for a long time for the party, or maybe had stored stuff from before the war so as to be able to celebrate in style.

I think we all felt that we would wake up the following morning to a bright new world, but nothing changed. It had been a few months since the last of the V2s had exploded; Mum's experience at Forest Gate had been one of the last. We had got used to going about our daily business without the interruption of war.

There was also some expectation that rationing would come to an end and there would be more goods in the shops. For that to be achieved the government had more important things to attend to, and most rationing carried on for a further five or six years.

In the summer of 1945, after the war had ended, the German troops were rounded up in Jersey and the remainder of the Channel Islands, which they had occupied since the beginning of the conflict and they were shipped back to Germany. The newsreels in the cinemas at that time carried pictures of them being marched to the docks and on to boats.

The fight with Japan had not been concluded and they carried on harassing our forces for a further three months. The end came on 6th August 1945, when the allies dropped the first atomic bomb to be used in a war on Hiroshima, one of their cities, destroying it completely. But they still would not surrender so three days later, on 9<sup>th</sup> August 1945, a further bomb was dropped on Nagasaki, again, totally destroying all that was there: buildings, roads, and no doubt, people; this brought an end to the fighting.

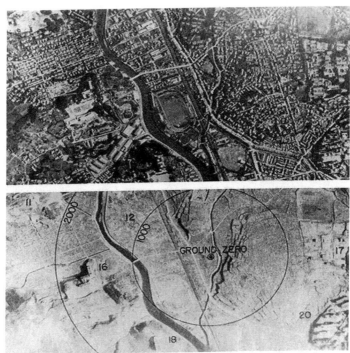

*The two pictures above are of Nagasaki: the top one showing how the city was before the 9th August 1945, the lower one after the bomb had been dropped.*

**

The new school and a new term in September 1947 came and I was in for a shock. Teachers which had been demobbed from the forces had taken control and new lessons were introduced; gymnastics, woodworking, metalwork and an art class in a room with a north facing roof light, so that there would be no shadows to spoil your work. I had now been moved to the Warren County Secondary Boys' School, which was right next door to the juniors where I had previously attended. All these tutorials were interesting and came in very useful in later years. For instance, we were taught the various uses of woodworking tools, and in another workroom understanding the difference between metals and how to harden a piece of steel. Artwork was always interesting especially instructions on how to set up a picture before you actually draw it.

Very quickly the school days were very different and so was the discipline. Assembly was held in the School Hall first thing in the morning, and one dare not be late. The teachers would stand on stage, prayers and hymns would be sung to the accompaniment of a piano, before the pupils were allowed to go off to their classes.

If you had done something the day before to cause the wrath of the school, then your name would be read out at assembly, I think that embarrassment only happened to me once. For the more serious offence it was to stand outside the headmaster's study and await his pleasure; if that was to use the cane on you then so be it, sometimes on the hand or maybe he would bend you over and whack your bottom.

Swimming lessons were introduced on a weekly basis, the school did not have a pool but there was one a few miles away in Dagenham. We would line up at the school gate with a rolled towel and our trunks inside, which we had brought from home, and file onto a beige and green Bedford Duplex coach − a real treat − far better than sitting in a class room. But then winter came and it was not so funny. The swimming pool had no roof, also no heating, and some days frost was still on the ground, but we were expected, and did get changed and go into the water. Brrrrrrr…

The previous year, without any training for it, I was informed I was to take an exam called 'The Eleven Plus'. Up to that period my input from the previous school and my keenness to learn anything, had been very poor. I was told that if I passed this exam then I would be eligible for Grammar School, which meant very little to me. I did not do very well; the questions on the exam papers were too difficult for my scant knowledge.

So as I said above, I was moved to the school next door, where to my surprise, I found myself in the top class of the year out of the four that existed. There were classes A, B and C, and because the school did not want a 'D' which could mean dunce, they named the top class Alpha, which was above the A, and that is where I found myself.

A few years later they gave me another chance at The Eleven Plus examination and called it 'The Thirteen Plus'. I think I did a little better but not enough to shine, but it cannot have been all that bad, because the school wrote to Father and offered me a place at a Grammar School, along with another lad.

At that time the school leaving age was 14. Dad, said 'No' to the idea of me being educated any longer, making it clear that I should go out to work the following year to earn a living. It did not work out that way, the National leaving age for schools was raised to 15 and I had to stay on for the extra year anyway.

Looking back I enjoyed that period of my life, although I could not get on with French. Why is 'door' masculine and 'window' a feminine noun, or is it the other way round? Also my English was a struggle. Today it would be recognised that I suffered from dyslexia, but at that time you just had to try harder, and in real terms that is what I have had to do since.

In one of the years at school our English lessons were taken by a young lady teacher, and at each period she asked us to find a new word and tell the class what it was on the next occasion. After a few times when I could not think of anything and was reprimanded for it, I consulted my sister, Frances, who was very good at languages. She taught me parrot fashion, 'onomatopoeia' which I practised over and over again until the next period of English.

On the day the teacher started going round the class, and various boys were giving her words, and she was saying good, how do you spell it and they would reply. Then it came to my turn, it was worth the surprised look on her face as I repeated what I had been practising, it was with doubt on her face when she asked me to spell it, and so I did. The class did not actually clap but I think they were impressed, the teacher said, "Very good," but then she said, "what does it mean?"

Now I did not think that was very fair because she had not asked anyone else that question, nor had she in previous lessons. I was stunned as I did not know the answer, I was told to tell her at the next period, and added, "Do not come up with another word unless you know what it means." I sat down feeling very stupid. (Roughly it means a word that is spelt like it sounds, for instance 'splash'.)

I have always struggled with English, what I did not realise, as I have already stated, that I was suffering from dyslexia, and as it was not something that was recognised, I continued to try harder. My spelling was always poor, but it did get better because I did not know that I had a problem. I am forever grateful to the people who invented the computer with spell check.

I was also very good at Gymnastics, in the last two years I appeared in a performance given by the school for parents to attend near to Christmas. I would, with others, during the interval give a gymnastic display doing somersaults, headstands and other movements on the restricted area of the stage. At least people clapped.

Technical drawing was something else that I shined at and was always near the top of the class in that subject. One reason is because I have perfect sight. One day I was leaning over the desk creating a technical drawing, I was aware the teacher was leaning over me. There was a line on the drawing I had to take another off of it at right angles. I measured where the line should start and without making a mark on the paper I drew the right angle. The teachers' reaction was, "You did not make a mark after you measured it, boy." He took a ruler and measured where I had started the line and it was in the perfect place. He now felt embarrassed and said, "You were lucky, in future put a dot after you have measured where it should start." Perhaps he was right but after I started my architectural business a long time after, I still did it my way and never got it wrong. But the school taught me a lot and what I learned stood me in good stead for later in life, especially when I undertook graphic work to earn a living.

**

When my second teeth started to grow they were crooked in the front and protruded over my bottom lip, with the result I was often called Goofy, which was after the Walt Disney Cartoon Character of that name. Even my own Father would use the term and another favourite of his was 'stupid'. I digress.

On the way home from school, like all children, we would play games and one of them would be to touch someone saying 'You're it' and start running and they would try and catch you to make you 'it'. We played this game on bikes.

One day after leaving the school we cycled home along Mill Lane which in itself leads into East Road. I leaned over to Dennis, who I was riding with, touched him on the arm shouting, 'You're it', and off I went.

The roads were always empty, as there was very little traffic and very few people owned cars. I swung into our turning with my head down, my legs whirring around on the pedals going very fast. With Dennis shouting 'stop' or something like that behind me.

Outside number 15 someone had parked a car. Dennis was still shouting which made me try to go faster as I was not taking any notice as I thought he wanted to catch up with me to make me 'it'.

There was an almighty bang as I hit the front bumper dead centre of the Ford 10, shown in the picture above. The Ford was the only car parked in the road which is about half a mile long. On the front of the car it had a small V- shaped motive on the top of the radiator, which my mouth hit carving a slice out of my lower lip and knocking two front teeth out, top and bottom. As I slid up and over the bonnet it made a long cut down my chest. My goofy days were over, and a big lesson learned to look where I'm going.

I think I was about twelve when this happened; certainly, it was the early days of the National Health Service which came into being in 1948. I was taken to hospital where they put 16 stitches to hold my bottom lip together − Father was pleased that there were no medical expenses to be met.

The owner of the car was very nice about it and told Dad and myself not to worry about the damage, which also pleased Father. But my bike was bent and buckled beyond repair. It was a long time before I could replace it. At that time I was doing a 'paper round' in the morning, which was about two miles long – without the bike I had to walk it carrying the papers in a sack over my shoulder.

**

During the war, food had been very scarce, and Mum used to make all sorts of odd meals to try and put some flavour in or make things more interesting. Homemade fish cakes – lovely, what was in them? I do not know and as fish was in short supply – probably not fish!

One day, shortly after the war, a canteen type van came into the street selling steak and kidney pies. These were delicious, he used to call once a week and I looked forward to that day with mouth-watering pleasure. I guess that is why I have been hooked on them ever since, but it is rare today to find a pie made perfect with the right amount of kidney to steak and a juicy gravy, just like those sold from that van, thinking about them as I write has my mouth-watering. But during the summer, Mother would not buy them because of the risk of infection. There was no facility to chill the produce so in the warm weather the bacteria may have developed while on the van and maybe they would cause a tummy upset.

On an occasion the family went to Southend-on-Sea for the day, getting there by a packed train with standing room only. Southend is famous for its long pier of over a mile long which allows boats to visit the area. Even at high tide it is possible to walk out a long way as the water is not very deep. I was paddling in the murky water, which was a little way above my ankles; the ground was firm but rippled made up of a very fine sandy/mud. Suddenly there was a very sharp pain in the centre of my right foot.

Lifting my foot from the water, which was starting to go red, I could see the jagged base of a broken bottle sticking out of my foot. I managed to pull it out and limped back to the family who were getting ready to go home. There was a queue at the nearby First Aid Post, so Dad decided that catching the train home was more important. He told me to stop being a cry baby and insisted that I put my shoes and socks on. But I don't think he realised how bad the cut was, perhaps if he had looked he would have known.

The train was packed and it was standing room only in the corridors. Somebody took pity on me and let me sit on their case; it was not until blood started seeping up my socks did my parents start taking it seriously. When we got home Mum cleaned and bandaged it and eventually it got better.

During all the time we lived in East Road, on a regular a basis, an agent from the Liverpool and Victoria Assurance Company, would call round to collect money for the life policies that my parents had taken out with him. On one visit he told them that he was leaving as he had bought a house and a shop in Ramsgate, on the Kent coast, and intended to run his new home as a B & B.

Dad booked a holiday with him for the following summer and on the due day we were full of excitement, as we had not had a holiday before. With packed suitcases and in a cheerful mood we made our way on foot to the train station, about two miles away to catch the first train. It was a difficult journey; two trains into central London and then the underground to Waterloo Station, before queuing for the packed train down to the coast. When we got off at Ramsgate Station we had to find our way, carrying heavy packed cases, to where we were to stay.

We were allotted the first floor of the house, Fran had her own bedroom, the other two rooms for my brother and I, and Mum and Dad in the front of the house.

For the first time in my life we were on holiday and could play on a beach. Coastal areas had been banned during the war years and travelling very limited so people did not have the opportunity to visit the sea.

On one of the days when we were on the beach, a bicycle bell was ringing, I looked up and saw a man coming along the promenade on a three-wheeled tricycle with a box to the front, on which was a sign saying 'stop me and buy one'. The man pedalling the machine was selling Walls Ice Cream, and Dad bought us one each. There was no cone, and only one flavour vanilla, to go with it just a grease proof paper wrapper. It was my first taste of ice cream and I still like it, something else I am hooked on.

It was the following year in 1948, when Mum and Dad bought a 1939 dark blue shining Austin Big 7, it was called big because it had two more doors than the normal model. When they brought it home it caused a lot of excitement in the street, as neighbours came out to admire the little car as very few of them owned such a thing. One of the reasons for buying it was my father did not want the horror of the train journey back to Ramsgate where he had booked the same house for the following year.

When we arrived in Ramsgate in the little car, we had expected the same arrangement for sleeping as the previous year. However, it was not to be, all five of us was to share the one front room. Dad was not having any of it, saying something like, 'It was not right for girls to sleep in the same room as the boys.' So we did not stay and got back into the car. Dad had seen a camping site on the way into town which had a sign saying 'Tents for hire'. We were shown a large bell type tent and for the following fortnight we tried our hand at camping, and the family liked it. For the following years holiday it was decided by my parents that is what we would do.

From a government surplus store my mum and dad bought a tent and other items to go camping. I could not have realised at the time I was going to spend a long time in the same type of tent, later in my life. With a trailer that Dad had borrowed fixed to the back of the car, which was as big as the vehicle itself, all of the camping gear was loaded into it and all five of us set off to tour Devon and Cornwall.

The little car's engine would struggle to get to 40 mph with only the driver in it, so with the load for this holiday its top speed was not much over thirty. With no motorways and its slow speed, it took three days to get to the West Country from our home in Essex. Sleeping in fields and cooking on a primus stove in the evenings.

The poor little car was not much good at hills either and on more than one occasion we had to get out and walk up while Dad coaxed the little thing with its trailer to the top, but sometimes it would need our help by all four of us pushing it.

When we arrived at Lynton in North Devon it refused the hill out of town. We were stuck on the side of the road where it doubled back on itself and was very steep. Every time we tried to move off the, clutch would slip and the car stayed where it was. After some time four burly men came along in a builder's lorry and they saw what the problem was, so they unhooked the trailer and attached it to their vehicle and off they went with all our possessions. We gave the car a push and off it went now the load had been lightened. Dad drove up and we walked up the steep incline where we found him waiting at the top of the hill with the trailer and then we were off on our adventures again.

It was a good holiday, travelling down as far as Land's End, sometimes staying in fields as there were not too many organised camp sites, and finally spending a few days in West Bay near Bridport in Dorset, before returning home.

It was around about this time my father introduced me to alcohol. He had to go to Romford, on some form of Union business and took me along as company in the Austin seven; it was the first year that I had worn long trousers. The business was conducted in a pub in Romford High Street and it was the first time I had been in a bar, as I stated earlier, children were not allowed in licensed premises. We were standing at the bar with this other man who Dad had gone to see, and he bought me a bottle of light ale. When the barmen went to pour it into a glass he stopped him from doing it. The glass and the full bottle were given to me and I poured the beer into the tumbler. Both the men thought it very funny and rolled up with laughter, when the beer frothed up out of the glass and over the bar. I just felt embarrassed. It was then they taught me how to pour beer properly.

**

It was on March 5th 1950 that my sister, Christine was born, and I was to leave school that year in the December, to start my working life.

The world was a much simpler place in that period, we were taught to be hardworking, trustworthy, also honest and respectful, not only at school but in the home and with one's peers. Using swear words was a serious offence, especially in front of women, I have seen men seriously remonstrated in a pub for using bad language in front of someone's wife.

Overall the last four years of school I excelled with each lesson and as the previous learning period had been abysmal, without the latter I would have been a dunce. But I think my school report on the following pages sums it up. But what it does not say was that the war years taught me to be self-sufficient also to make do and mend, and when things are hard, then try harder to overcome the problem.

*Before continuing with my story – a few nouns and how they were used in the 1950s:*

- *Pasta had not been invented. Curry was a surname.*
- *A 'take away' was a mathematical problem.*
- *A 'Pisa' was something to do with a leaning tower.*
- *Bananas and oranges only appeared at Christmas time.*
- *All 'crisps' were plain; the only choice we had was whether to put the salt on or not.*
- *A 'Big Mac' was what we wore when it was raining.*
- *Oil was for lubricating, fat was for cooking*
- *Tea was made in a teapot using tea leaves.*
- *Coffee was Camp, and came in a bottle.*
- *Cubed sugar was regarded as posh.*
- *Only Heinz made beans.*
- *Fish didn't have fingers in those days.*
- *None of us had ever heard of 'yoghurt'.*
- *Healthy food consisted of anything edible.*
- *Cooking outside was called camping.*
- *Seaweed was not a recognised food.*
- *'Kebab' was not even a word, never mind a food.*
- *Sugar enjoyed a good press in those days, and was regarded as being white gold.*
- *Surprisingly, Muesli was readily available, it was called cattle feed.*
- *Pineapples came in chunks in a tin; we had only ever seen a picture of a real one.*
- *Water came out of the tap, if someone had suggested bottling it and charging more than petrol for it they would have become a laughing stock.*
- *The one thing that we never ever had on our meal table in the fifties was elbows!*

## ESSEX EDUCATION COMMITTEE.
### BOROUGH OF DAGENHAM.

School  The Warren County Secondary Boys'

Postal Address  Whalebone Lane N. Chadwell Heath.

Date  21st December 1950

      Percy Chatley has attended this School since September 1947, and during that time he has proved himself to be a thoroughly honest, hardworking and trustworthy lad.

      He is a most intelligent pupil, and has made splendid progress in all his classwork. Though all his work is good, special mention should be made of his work in Mathematics and Physical Training, in which subjects he is very proficient.

      He has very pleasing manners, and his behaviour and attendance has been most satisfactory.

      For the last 6 months he has acted as a School Prefect, in which capacity he has carried out some very useful services.

      I regard him as one of our most satisfactory pupils, and it is with great confidence that I can recommend him for employment.

                               Head Master.

# Leaving School

So off to work I go. I am not certain how I got employment at the Plessey Company; I think the school and my father had something to do with it. The company had by this time moved from the Eastern Avenue to a large factory in Ley Street, Ilford. I can vaguely remember an interview with my father being present, but I felt so out of touch with this grown up world.

There was a ground floor office in a parade of shops, on a corner of one of the side turnings opposite the factory; this was where the employment officer interviewed new staff. I attended there sometime in December to discuss being employed for the first time, and the official agreed that I should start immediately after the New Year to be taught electronics. I was told to start at eight in the morning and given details of where to go. Prior to going, my thoughts were one of pride and the fact I was being offered a career in the up-and-coming world of electrical engineering, so I was looking forward to what I thought would be a great day.

The first morning I arrived with a deep feeling of trepidation, similar to how I felt when I took The Eleven Plus. I entered the factory. I was to be trained as an apprentice electronics engineer at seven pence and a farthing an hour. In today's money that is less than three pence an hour. (*In an old pound there were 240 pence, a farthing was worth a quarter of a penny, so there were 960 farthings to a pound, or today a*

*farthings value .00104 new pence., which equates to 2.401*
*pence per hour when I first started work). To put this into*
*context – a telephone call cost two pence – fish and chips four*
*pence – a loaf of bread 1.5 pence – 12 eggs 8.5 pence – a*
*Man's suit 10 pounds – a new Ford car 80 pounds – a semi-*
*detached house 750pounds, and a terraced one half that price.*

I lasted less than a week, much to my father's
disappointment. I had expected to start being taught about
electronics, but the reality was very different. I was introduced
to a shop floor where there were rows of women sitting at
benches, all of them soldering joints on mother boards, the
heart of the television sets being produced by the factory.

In front of each person on a bench there was a soldering
iron with a square copper head which was heated over a gas
flame. Every so often the irons would burn and go black
making them useless for the work the girls were doing. My job
was to collect the burnt irons and replace them with fresh ones.
I would take the useless ones to a bench grinder, grind the
black part off the head of the iron back to its shiny copper, and
then return it to one of the benches and change it for another
useless one.

There were a lot of busy women in overalls sitting in rows
on stalls, which I took a lot of stick from. Lots of irons and
only me running around trying to keep up, if one of the girls
could not work because her iron was useless then they would
lose pay. I was expected to supply my own work clothes, and I
was only allowed one break at lunch time which was very hard
after my time at school, where the period is broken more
frequently. After a few days I had had enough. So I went back
to the corner office and gave them the news and started
looking for another job, little knowing that the Plessey
Company was going to feature in my life again. Perhaps I
should have stayed waiting on their pleasure to train me as an
engineer, who knows where that would have led.

Next was another apprentice position: this time as an electrician, but in real terms only working as a mate as there was no college theory, just practical work. One got the feeling they called you an apprentice so they could pay you less money – that thought is the cynic coming out in me. The wages were slightly more than the factory; also the work was a lot more interesting as we travelled around the East End of London to various sites. At one time I was cycling 15 miles twice a day to the centre of London and back, working on a large site just off Piccadilly Circus. The company I was working for were the electrical contractors on a new build, replacing a building that had been badly damaged during the war and converting it to a restaurant and also a night club. After about a year the work dried up and I was again looking for employment.

In 1952, for a seventeen-year-old, jobs were few and far between because of the compulsory two-year National Service for boys when they reached the age of eighteen, which for me was not too far away. I started working for Odeon Cinemas as a mate to the maintenance engineer's. We travelled around the different theatres in East London carrying out repairs and other work as required.

In early 1953 I was cycling through Wanstead in East London when I saw in a parade of shops an Army Recruiting Office. I parked the bike against the wall and went in where a sergeant sat me down to discuss my future in the forces. There were various options from three years to twenty-five years to sign up for, I decided on the smallest of them.

Once the Army had accepted that I was for them, they required me to take a medical. I arrived one morning to find there were about another 30 men who were also joining up. We were put into a line and stood in front of a doctor, well I assumed he was a doctor, he checked our chests and then the line moved on. We were told to roll our left shirt sleeve up, another orderly/nurse walked along the line with a needle which he pricked the skin at the top of your arm without changing the instrument between each man. After which the line moved on again into another room where we were told to drop our trousers and a doctor/nurse had a very good feel around our private parts, all very embarrassing.

It was a great relief to be accepted as I would not have the worry of looking for work for the next three years. At seventeen and a half, the earliest one could join the regular forces, I joined the Corps of Royal Engineers on a three-year engagement as 22952361 Sapper Chattey.

March 1953 arrived. The evening before was quite emotional saying my goodbyes to the family, and to my surprise my mother and father gave me a camera which I was very proud of, which taught me a sharp lesson because it was stolen a few days after arriving at the first Army camp I was to stay in. The journey to get from East London to the little town of Abergavenny in mid Wales was not an easy task as none of the steam trains were particularly quick, and it involved about six changes and took most of the day. I finally arrived at this quaint little place in the early evening; I was impressed when I found an Army truck waiting for me outside the station.

I do not know what I expected when I joined up but there were a few surprises, I think the first was the wearing of the stiff khaki serge trousers, they took some getting used to especially when wet. The other was going to bed without sheets, just a rough blanket, suddenly three years seemed a very long time.

After the initial 'intake' camp I was posted to Aldershot for Corps training, which involves marching and cleaning to get one in the frame of mind to understand and obey orders. *(Get your chin up – swing those arms – stamp your feet etc., etc.)* After a period of about six weeks it was off to another camp for engineering training, building bridges, digging trenches and even how to handle a landing craft – now that was interesting. But the bridge building was hard, we concentrated for five whole days building Bailey Bridges across gullies, although we had instructions on how to build them, nobody had said beforehand how heavy each piece of the structure was.

In this period the Army made me very fit. On the way home going on the short leaves that I was allowed, I thought it was fun and would think nothing of running up the down escalator at the Bank underground station in London, in Army boots and a serge uniform with a case − that is not easy. As you get near to the top you dare not slow up, otherwise you are going down which makes it just that much harder.

Standing Orders are published each day on notice boards, they need to be read, otherwise something important could be missed, and you would be in trouble. It was no use relying on others to read the board as they would think it very funny if you got a dressing down for not doing something that was on orders. One day I learned I had been posted to Gillingham in Kent for further training, this time in communications.

Why the Army thought I would be good at communication I do not know. I was not too happy when one of the first things we were told on the course was that the average life of a signalman in a war zone was twelve minutes. The itinerary taught us all about wireless technology and field craft in the operation of a units signal office. We also frequently went out on field practice and on one occasion just before the training came to an end, we were given maps and shown an area which was near the Hogs Back outside Basingstoke in southern England, which was a long way from Gillingham in Kent.

There were in all about twelve vehicles in the convoy to reach the destination each one fitted for wireless. I was in the second 15cwt truck next to the driver, and was supposed to be map reading but I was very happy following the first vehicle who was leading the way. We came to a town in the middle of which there was a set of traffic lights. The lights started to change to red, the leading vehicle carried on, which left me holding a map in my hand and not the slightest knowledge of where we were.

The lights eventually changed to green far too quickly for me, as I was still trying to work out what part of the country we were in. I told the driver to go straight on trying to follow where the other one had gone but they were out of sight. I was looking around for some sign which would give me a clue to our whereabouts, and behind us the Army convoy continued totally believing everything was right. I was still in difficulties when we came to a 'T' Junction. The driver said, "Which way?" In front of me was a sign saying Brighton and an arrow pointing to the left. Not knowing where the Hogs Back was, although knowing it was not near to the coast − I thought to myself that we needed to go in the opposite direction.

Now the Brighton road was very busy, and I decided to turn right which meant crossing two lines of traffic. A break appeared in the stream of vehicles and we were off dutifully followed by all the others. It was then I found out where we were, my heart sank we should have gone the other way. I think the reader can probably imagine, all these Army wagons trying to turn round amongst streams of holiday traffic, to go in the opposite direction. The dressing down I got by the commanding officer when we finally got to our destination is not worth recording.

It was early December when my time and training in Gillingham came to an end. I was given a week's embarkation leave and then I was off to Kenya, leaving about eight days before Christmas.

# The Army

When I joined the Forces I was very lucky on two counts. Firstly, if I had joined a week earlier, the unit I would have been assigned to, had to spend four months training, come rain or shine as they practised marching for the Queen's Coronation in June of that year. Whilst it would have been a proud thing to do, but it would not have been very funny, especially on the actual day standing for hours in one spot lining the road waiting for the Coronation Coach.

The second reason: the cold and muddy Korean War was in full swing and I could very easily have been posted there, instead I was off to sunnier climbs to try and help quell the Mau Mau. The Engineering Regiment I was posted to had already arrived in Kenya where it was to build roads through the forests and plains so that the security forces could move around quickly.

It was another early start, I needed to travel for most of one day to get from Chadwell Heath to Barton Stacey in Hampshire, which is near Andover. A few days later I found myself sitting in a railway carriage with wooden seats, in Stratford Marshalling Yards in East London, which is about four miles from home where I had started from.

We, that is the troop I was stationed with, spent a number of hours in the goods yard being shunted around various parts of it. Then the train, with our unit sitting uncomfortably inside, made its way through North London. It was another surprise when after leaving the train and getting on to more Army lorries we arrived at RAF Stansted.

Today Stansted is a major airport to the north of London, but in 1953 it was an airfield where RAF bomber planes were stationed protecting the country against Communism − with old Nissan huts left over from the Second World War. To our amazement we were led to an Avro York airliner which was to take us to Africa. I say surprised because in the period when the Cold War was at its height, (although another seven years would pass before the Eastern Block built the Berlin Wall separating east from West) troop movements were on the secret list and not broadcast, anyway I think the Army took great delight in surprising you.

At that time very few people had flown, holiday travel was more likely to be a trip on a coach or train to the seaside. This was so different, a real adventure, I had the privilege of being the first person in our family to fly in a plane. At that time most troops were moved around the world by ship which took up a lot of time, if we had gone to Africa by that method it would have taken about four weeks.

The York as shown in the picture on the previous page, rumbled along the runway and we were airborne. Now this plane was nothing like the jets that we know of today, its four engines driving large propellers vibrated throughout the aircraft, the vibrations only equal to the amount of noise they made, making it impossible to speak without shouting in the other person's ear.

It was to take three days to get to Nairobi, the capital of Kenya. We were told the plane had no navigational equipment as a result of which it could not fly at night, and as it had no air conditioning to supply oxygen, not very high either and always below the cloud level. In the entire journey we could clearly see what was happening on the ground. I'm sure the pilot navigated using road maps.

Our first stop was Malta. We were transferred by antique buses to a very nice hotel on the coast, where we had dinner and a walk along the beach before retiring to a comfortable bedroom where we stayed the night. After breakfast we were bussed back to the aircraft and off to a very sunny and hot El Alamein, for a refuelling stop. At the airport, which was in the middle of the desert, there was a shop and a place for refreshments. As we got off the aircraft the heat hit us in the face, how our forces coped with that in the Second World War when the Desert Rats were fighting against Rommel's German forces, it must have been very difficult.

We followed the Nile through Egypt where we could see the pyramids, and on to Khartoum, arriving on Christmas Day. The city was in turmoil with rioting factions, and the powers that be did not want English soldiers to be seen. The result of which was we wore civilian jackets and were bedded down in some form of hall, on the floor with straw paillasses and a blanket for comfort.

On leaving Khartoum we had to have another refuelling stop in Uganda so the aircraft had adequate fuel to climb to the airport at Nairobi, which is at about 5500 feet above sea level or nearly 2000 metres. The picture on the previous page was taken on the runway side of the Terminal Building at Nairobi Airport – the arm at the top reads 4245 miles to London. *(Sorry about the stain, it is where it has not been developed properly, probably my fault.)*

In late December 1953 and after spending a few more uncomfortable nights on straw mattresses, we climbed onto the back of yet more Army lorries, and were taken over bumpy rutted dirt roads for about one hundred and twenty miles north of the city. The new camp was already under construction by the previous arrivals, who had travelled by ship. The site of this facility was about thirty miles south from the Equator. Because of the ground level being of more than six thousand feet above sea level, the weather was more akin to England without the cold winters. More details of Kenya in a short while.

**

Mombasa, on the Kenyan Indian Ocean coast, is also just south of the equator and very hot. It was two years later when our unit arrived there with the rest of the regiment.

I had been there twice before on holiday with some of the lads. This time we boarded the TSS Captain Cook to be taken home to the UK. The ship was on its return journey to Southampton after taking immigrants to New Zealand

We travelled in style, four guys to a cabin, waiter service at meal times and food that would not have gone amiss in any restaurant. The ship took three weeks to sail up the Indian Ocean, through the Red Sea and the Suez Canal, across the Mediterranean past Gibraltar, and up the Atlantic to Southampton and home. A nice ride; it would have cost a fortune if we had had to pay.

T.S.S. "CAPTAIN COOK"

We had no Army duties to do on board. However, it was my responsibility to go round the deck where the troops I was in charge off had been assigned to, and wake everyone at 7.00 o'clock. The officers in charge of the ship were not going to let anyone lay in bed all day.

The ship docked at various ports en route, one was Aden where we were allowed to go ashore. It was a hot dusty place similar to Suez which is at the other end of the Red Sea and the Suez Canal. We also left the ship there for a day's walkabout and it is the first place where I saw Arabs playing spot the ball. They hide one under three beakers and quickly move them about and they bet you cannot guess which one it is under. Yes, I fell for it at a cost which hurt my pocket and my pride.

One day whilst on deck I had laid down in the shade in a quiet spot in a corner for a snooze, it was very hot. I woke up in terrible pain and looking down at my chest there was a large blister covering the whole of it where the sun had burned me.

When I had gone to sleep I had not put a thought to the ship changing course and my shade going. This was a big problem. I did not dare go to the medical officer because the Army sees it as a serious offence to injure yourself. So I kept it quiet and after a few days of agony the blister finally went down leaving my chest red and raw.

**

All of which was two years after we had first arrived in the country. The journey to the north of Nairobi, after arriving from England was to a little village called Nyeri, which consisted of a few shops and native huts. To the edge of town were some colonial type houses with beautiful manicured gardens behind high walls. The camp we were posted to was about four miles from the outskirts of the village.

The village is also famous for The Tree Tops Hotel which was built in the branches of a very large 300-hundred-year-old Ficus tree. The year before we arrived, on the 5th February 1952, Princess Elizabeth and the Duke of Edinburgh were staying overnight, at the Hotel, where she was informed of the death of her father, King George VI, and she became Queen. The hotel was later burned down by terrorists, as a publicity stunt, because it was very famous and their excuse was that it had been used as a lookout post for the Kenya Police.

The village also has another claim to fame; it is where Lord Baden-Powell founder of the Scout movement is interred along with his wife.

The area has yet another story for it is not too far from the village where the Adamson's looked after animals, especially lions, which prompted the best-selling novel *'Born Free.'* In the mid-sixties the novel was made into a blockbuster film of the same name starring Virginia McKenna, which, in turn, formed the animal charity in the early nineties with a similar name.

The area is very central to where the Mau Mau operated. Most of the unmade roads that lead into the hills and forest where mainly white people had made a living had become overgrown with vegetation after the farmers had left in fear of being slaughtered by the terrorists. The Regiment's job was to open these roads so they could be used by the security forces and in some cases build new ones.

From Wikipedia:

*The Mau Mau Uprising, which began as a protest in 1951 and 1952 of British dominance and discrimination in the Kikuyu homeland, quickly became a violent uprising. It was suppressed by the British over the period 1953−1954. In 1953, the Aberdare forest provided refuge to many hundreds of Mau Mau rebels, led by Dedan Kimathi. In June 1953, the entire region was declared off-limits for Africans, and orders to shoot Africans on sight were set in place. A major military operation in late 1953 ("Operation Blitz") left 125 guerrillas dead. This was followed in January 1954 by "Operation Hammer", led by the King's African Rifles. As a protest against the shoot on sight orders, and repeated military action, Mau Mau rebels burnt down the Treetops Hotel (which acted as a lookout for the King's African Rifles) on 27 May 1954 in a contentious 'military action' or 'act of terror'. The incident took place as the uprising was slowly being brought to an end by British military action.*

# On Active Service

When we arrived we had to laugh as it was called Ellis Camp, Nyeri, and all we could see were a few marquees and some tents and a large area of open grass, no gate or fencing. It was on high ground about four miles from the village, surrounded by forest. There was no barrier between us and the trees and until one was installed, a few months later. We all felt a little uncomfortable sleeping in tents with nothing between us and the open countryside, and no doubt the terrorists.

Two Regiments were assigned to the camp, one being 74 Field Park Squadron of the 39 Corps Royal Engineers to which I was posted in HQ Company. There were four companies, each had four troops containing forty men; most of which were away in the field carrying out construction work. We kept in touch with them on a daily basis by a radio link. The other unit was of the REME (*Royal Electrical & Mechanical Engineers*) who supplied the plant – bulldozers and other items for the construction work. Eventually there were hundreds of men living in tents in the twin community, whilst others lived in units of about forty men that were out in the remote areas building roads.

In due course there were tented workshops, offices and near the main gate, a corrugated tin hut, RHQ (*Regimental Head Quarters*) wireless room, where I started work. The rest of the offices were in marquees, so we lads in communications were privileged to be in the dry, especially when it rained and it could do so very heavily. We had a dry concrete floor whilst the other office staff would have mud at their feet.

One thing I could not escape from was guard duty; everybody had to do it. The first time was scary, there were twelve of us and that meant four men on duty in pairs for two hours and then four hours off. The idea was those on duty walked around the perimeter of the camp in single file. One pair one way the other pair going in the opposite direction. One evening it was my turn and with this other fellow, in the pitch dark and no fences just a well-worn path to follow.

In the woods to our right I could see lots of lanterns moving about and the more I looked the more there were. I caught up with the other lad and pointed them out to him, my heart racing thinking that we were being attacked by hordes of Mau Mau all carrying lanterns. He didn't actually laugh at me but called me a silly something or other as the lanterns were nothing more than fire flies.

**

We, that is the individuals in the Army, had the opportunity to go on farm guard. The Mau Mau was very reluctant to engage in combat with the English forces and very rarely did, the settlers felt safer with a couple of soldiers billeted on their property.

I say farm, for these properties is not really the right word, they were very large estates, and it could take half an hour to drive up their driveway, which would have miles and miles of crops on either side which the settlers were growing, most of it coffee plants, although there was others as I remember, pineapple comes to mind.

They were small communities with a house for the farmer and his family. Close by would be rows of native built huts which would be the dwellings for the African workers and their families. The whole estate would be completely self-contained with no communications of any sort. The first one I stayed in had a generator for electricity, powerful enough to give lighting as well as power. The second farm where I stayed, the electricity produced was just for power, lighting was by oil lamps.

I had the opportunity to go twice, with another Army lad, and live in the house and eating fabulous food and wine at the same table as the host. It also made a lovely break sleeping with sheets next to you, and having your washing and cleaning done. At meal times my place was facing the door from the kitchen but to one side on the opposite side of the table. In front of me laid out by the African waiters and lying on a white covering, the silver knives and forks besides which I would put an army .38 pistol close to my right hand, in case the terrorists tried to enter the room by following the waiters in. I would have an uninterrupted line of fire to them.

The settlers, some of whom had a generation or two behind them since their families had arrived in Kenya, lived in style. They also had busy lives growing crops, mainly coffee, with hundreds of acres to farm.

In their homes there were servants to cook and clean, waiters serving every meal on polished tables with silver and the best china. It sounds very grand but the estates were large and without staff they would not have functioned. The settlers' lifestyle was very lonely, as there were few visitors or other people to talk to except your close family and always the fear of being attacked. And, of course, no television *(in the fifties TV in England was very limited),* in Kenya they did have a radio which produced a crackly reception which was difficult to understand.

The settlers' fear was very real as many had been murdered by the terrorists. Their method was to secretly recruit waiters and kitchen staff belonging to the Kikuyu tribe, of which the Mau Mau were born members.

*A settlers' fortified home – note the block work around the windows.*

The easiest time to enter the home was at meal times when the family would all be in one place. The staff, some of whom had been employed by the owners for a long time and were trusted by the farmer. Unknown to the owner their employees' families would be threatened by the murderous terrorists threatening to kill them if they would not do their bidding. So under strong duress they would unlock the doors to the fortified house to let them in.

The invaders would have been waving Pangas as they entered the premises. (*A heavy, broad-bladed, long knife used for cutting a path through a thickly wooded forest*). As explained above they would follow the waiters as they left the kitchen to serve food in the dining room. Once in the room, they would slash their weapons through the air before attacking and killing everyone in the room. The house staff would disappear with the Mau Mau after trashing the house and stealing its valuables. Sometimes they would set light to the property so that it would burn to the ground, but not always as this would inform the security forces of what had taken place.

**

As already stated we went on holiday to Mombasa a couple of times, it was a long slow train journey from Nairobi. Although only about two hundred and something miles it took twenty-four hours sitting on wooden seats, with frequent long stops.

Mombasa was so very different to Nyeri and the mountains, it is on the east African coast about fifty or so miles from the Equator and bathed in constant sunlight with warm balmy evenings, and golden sandy beaches. We stayed in a hotel where the bedroom had no glass in the windows, just some form of grass rush matting hanging across the opening. The food was very good and it was the first time I tasted curry. I found it strange as it had different types of fresh fruit in a container to the side, all very nice.

As I explained earlier my upbringing did not encourage mixing with the opposite sex. Now here in Mombasa it was so very different and there was plenty to do in the evenings. When I had visited pubs or clubs back home, the boys stayed together and one did not approach a girl unless it was at a dance or you were introduced. Here was very different. For the first time in my life, because of the heat the women were scantily dressed, nothing like the demure dresses girls wore in the fifties in the UK.

At one venue the music was playing and the drinks were flowing, there were four of us in the party and there was a sign above a door which lead off the bar and read 'Massage' which created a load of interest. After a lot of bantering the group dared me to go in. Full of all types of funny feelings, I got up and walked towards the door, the others quickly followed.

There was a line of young girls, I guess in their teens, and each individual was invited to choose one.

The one you chose took you by the hand and led you to a small scruffy room with a dirt floor. There was a bowl of hot soapy water on the side which puzzled me for a moment – but she needed to do an inspection which was far more thorough and exciting than the medical version in Wanstead where I had applied to join the army.

The second time we went, we were staying at another hotel on the sea front. The owner of which had a small old Morris Cowley truck which he needed to be taken to Nairobi, so Ted, my Army companion and I volunteered to drive it back for him. Far better than the train journey.

It was and may still be a long dirt road. *(In Kenya it is called 'Murrum' I think that is the right spelling, it is red in colour and gives off thick dust behind the vehicle as it travels.)* The vehicle had a top speed of a little over 40 mph, with no load on the rear to dampen the hard springs coupled with the ruts on the road surface, it was a very bumpy ride. The truck itself was noisy, vibrated and rattled as it went along so it was not the most comfortable of journeys, but better than the train.

We had covered about one hundred miles, the sun had gone down, and the only light was from very dim headlights. We were very tired with all the movement and noise in the lorry and were pleased to see the lights of a little village, which was in the middle of nowhere off to the side of the road. So we turned into a track which was a little worse than the one we had been on, and stopped outside a store for a break. It was a scruffy general store with a corrugated tin roof, which appeared to sell everything. We wanted a drink but passed on the coffee, the cups did not look that clean, we also decided to wait until we got to Nairobi before eating as the food was not very appetising, neither were the utensils. To say 'grubby' would be an understatement, we left after drinking a coke out of a can.

We rattled our way out of the village and along the road when suddenly there was a loud noise from the engine. On inspection we found that a sparking plug had dropped out, in all the years of motoring before and since I have never known it to happen again.

We then had a problem. We are sitting in the wilds of Africa, no fire arms to protect ourselves, all sorts of wild animals roaming around, and an engine that needed some TLC. We tossed a coin to see who would walk back to the village to try and buy a sparking plug or to find some help. It was down to me to do the walking.

The surprise was that this small general store had the missing part which I bought and started to walk back. I had the torch with me which we had found in the truck. Whilst walking back, which took the best part of an hour, I was flashing the torch to see what was in front of me when I saw two white legs standing on the side of road, about one hundred yards away.

I stood there for some time, they did not move and no way was I going up there to find out who or what it was.

I turned round and made my way back to the village, where to my joy I found some men who had a convoy of new Peugeot cars to deliver to Nairobi from the docks at Mombasa. One of them gave me a lift back to the stranded vehicle. Ted was very pleased to see me, although he did get a fright when we pulled up in the car, it had been the only vehicle he had seen all night.

Oh yeah! The white legs? They turned out to be two posts marking a gully on the side of the road.

Ellis Camp was a tented community with the exception of the radio room which I described earlier. The tents in the camp were in groups arranged in lines and separated into Troops. There were five Companies belonging to the Regiment, I was in HQ and each company had four troops which were stationed out in the country on construction or other work. Each tent slept four men and over the canvas there was a fly sheet to help keep out the heat and the cold also to prevent water entering when it rained; they were also identical to the one we went camping round Devon and Cornwall many years before with the family. But that is not surprising as Dad had bought it from an ex-army store.

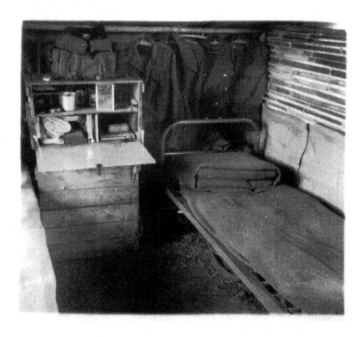

Each dwelling was fourteen feet by fourteen feet square, or four point three metres by four point three metres. Four men to a tent, each with his own corner, mine is shown below. It is an early picture with a dirt floor, later we managed to find floor boards from somewhere to make it more comfortable. The unit standing beside the bed I made from old boxes. Talking of comfort the mattress in the picture was filled with straw and tended to wear very thin, but it was something one got used to.

**

The Army likes to keep you fit, and besides marching and other exercises there was also an assault course which helps in keeping the muscles working. On one of these occasions we set off and after a long morning hike with full gear including a heavy rifle, we came to a wide, deep fast flowing river. On the far side there was a substantial rope attached to a thick branch of a very tall tree overhanging the water. It was the method for our unit to cross the river by hanging on to it and swinging to the other side.

My turn came and I had not been studying how the others had achieved the crossing without going into the water. There was the rope and a length of string attached to the bottom to pull it back so the next person could swing across. I stepped to the side of the muddy river bank, grabbed the rope and stepping off the bank I swung across. But I had the string between my legs instead of the outside of them by my ankle.

When I reached the far bank I could not get off the rope as the lads on the other side, who thought it very funny, had started to pull the string and the rope was now firmly between my knees and I started to swing back across the water.

There was only one thing I could do and that was to drop off as near the bank as possible in deep cold muddy water up to my waist also trying to keep my rifle out of the dirty liquid by holding it above my head. The bank was thick with mud but I managed to struggle up the slippery slope feeling very embarrassed.

**

Because the Mau Mau created hides in the jungle-like thick woodlands, the security forces banned all Africans from the forest; there were no fences; the lines were drawn on a map using grid references, which made an area 'OUT of BOUNDS' with an occasional sign fixed to a tree. Anything that moved within the box was fair game to be shot at, or if the RAF were involved, bombed.

I very rarely went out on patrol, and because of my duties in the radio room I normally did not get to go on assault courses as described in the previous paragraph. On one particular occasion there was a flap on and I was the guy carrying the two-way communications. A few days earlier a new inexperienced second Lieutenant had arrived in Kenya and was leading the patrol of about fifteen men. He was probably very good at map reading but where there are only trees and no land marks it adds a new dimension to the skill and in this instance he was not very good at it. It was a strange environment. We had been following a path which came to an end after which there were only trees and undergrowth, and our man at the front got lost which resulted in us crossing the line that defined the box.

The forest was very thick and we were using Panga style knives to cut our way through, when we heard the planes. Our movement through the 'out of bounds' area had been noted, probably because the wildlife – like our feathered friends which had been disturbed by our presence and had flown away in droves. This would have been seen by the *'lookout post'* searching the vast area for any sign of disturbance which could mean an illegal movement, who in turn would call an aircraft to the disturbance. Thank the Lord they were not very good at aiming either, but they were close and the explosions were all around us. The trees were protecting us, a sharp reminder of the Blitz in London. Unfortunately I could not get a signal on the radio to report our predicament.

Later that day we did discover the camp where the terrorists had recently been. They had constructed lean to shelters and it was amazing how they had cleared the undergrowth and yet had retained the cover of the trees to protect them from aerial photography.

**

In the autumn of 1954 I was posted to GHQ (*General Head Quarters*) in Nairobi, to operate the one and only link to the regiment for ordering stores and making reports to the centre of operations. This facility I had to operate was the only way GHQ and my previous unit could communicate securely. It was a one man operation, and as I liked working on my own it suited me perfectly.

Leaving the tented home and moving to very comfortable accommodation, living well and with my own Dhobi (*washing*) boy, who not only made my bed with clean sheets every day but also at the same time took my clothes for washing bringing my laundry back perfectly ironed − which was great, I liked the lifestyle.

There was more than that; a whole city and two safari parks to explore, a night life with others in the unit to enjoy and the weather a lot kinder than in the mountains.

My Army 19 Model Wireless Set in the picture below was first developed in the Second World War. This particular model has an extra power unit on the top to boost the outgoing signal. The image is taken in my own office in GHQ. I used the machine every day receiving coded reports or requests for stores, in Morse code from the Regiment. Morse code was a system I was taught while in Kenya and I became very proficient with it sending and receiving about sixty words a minute, the speed only determined by the speed the person could write the message when receiving it.

One request I remember quite clearly, was an order from the Regiment for antifreeze. The reply from GHQ was 'What do you want antifreeze for, you are only a few miles from the equator?' The explanation was that the vehicles who were working clearing the forest and making roads on Mount Kenya *(which has a snow peak all year round)*, their drivers had to drain the radiators every evening to prevent the engines from freezing overnight.

The picture of Mount Kenya was taken from my tent in Nyeri; the forest can be seen below the peaks. A troop of the Regiment was working in that area; at that height it is possible to put your hand in boiling water as the boiling point is very low because of the thin atmosphere.

The work I was doing was very important and secret so it was not well known because it was vital that the terrorists did not get to know of its existence. The traffic between the Regiment and GHQ could be either in plain language or in code which I would change into English unless it was marked top secret. The link between the two units was open twice a day first thing in the morning and then again in the late afternoon. One day around lunch time, I was walking back to my billet when the Sergeant Major stopped me and told me to follow him. He had been rounding up personnel and putting them on a lorry. There was some kind of event taking place in a hall outside of GHQ and they needed bodies to make sandwiches for a buffet.

I tried to explain to the NCO that I could not go because I had to be available later in the afternoon, but he would not listen and ordered me to get on the truck. When we arrived at the venue he singled me out, I guess because I had been difficult, to slice onions, and there was a big pile of them and as soon as I started cutting them tears started to roll down my face.

I was in a quandary I did not dare ignore the direct order of the superior officer and stop what I was doing, and yet time was passing to when I should be opening the rear link. The officer I dealt with at GHQ was a Major St John – there I was in this sort of shelter with tears running down my face when he walked by. He did a double take and asked me what I was doing there. I explained to him what happened, he nodded his head and pointing to his Land Rover and told me to tell his driver to take me back to my office, saying that he would deal with the Sergeant Major.

**

From time to time we could hire a Land Rover for the day from the Army's vehicle pool to go round the safari parks. There were two such parks on the outskirts of the capital city of Kenya. In the picture below we are leaving one of them, the Nairobi National Park. A few times we went around them looking at the wild life. I think we were charged about 25 pence, in today's English money, for the use of the vehicle for the day which included the fuel and an African driver.

The lads in GHQ knew everything and everyone, a few of us were having a drink in a bar when I was introduced to some of the RAF airmen. After a few bottles of White Label, the local beer, an invitation followed to go on one of their missions in a Lancaster Bomber over the forest. The aircraft was equipped for taking aerial pictures, which were used to try and discover terrorist camps, but they were also bombing anything that looked odd and shouldn't be there. A great day and well entertained but I could not help wondering if it was the same crew that had dropped bombs when the troop I was with got lost in the forest.

There was a servicemen's club not very far from GHQ, the Military Policemen who had an office near mine frequently invited me along there for Bingo Games. I had been there one evening and after the M.P.s had left, to go home to where they lived in married quarters with their families. I was feeling a little depressed because I had been informed earlier that my tour in GHQ was to come to an end. I was lucky in some respects because it should have only lasted three months but for some reason I was not called back to the regiment until after six months.

I had visited a few bars and as it was getting late I decided to get a taxi back to my quarters. Outside where I had been drinking, totally on my own, there was a lay-by where the taxis would wait. As I left I could see there was only one car and as I started to cross the road to go to it I saw another soldier running towards it. We arrived at the same time I on one side opening the rear door, he opening the opposite door. We both looked at each other in surprise, he said 'Percy Chattey!' and I said 'Harry Lark!'

I cannot say Harry was a friend but we knew each other from our school days although we were in different classes and he lived further down East Road. He was doing his National Service and was billeted in a camp in the opposite direction to GHQ, but nevertheless after his invitation to a game of cards with some of his mates I agreed to join them. It was very early in the morning when I finally got back to my bed, resulting in a struggle the following day to operate the link back to the Regiment. The funny thing about it was, I had not seen Harry since we had left school and I have not seen him since.

*Party Time at Camp Ellis in Nyeri*

# Year Two in Kenya

So it was goodbye to all the friends I had made in GHQ, and climbing into the back of the lorry, for the six hour journey back to Nyeri and Ellis Camp. The first thirty miles of the journey to Thicka, was not too bad as the road had a tarmac surface after which it became very rutted and dusty. Following another vehicle was the worst as the dust created by its wheels hung in the air and smothered everything.

On my return I was promoted one step up the Army's ladder and the real joy of that was my rifle was taken from me and I was issued with a Sten Gun. The best way to describe it is a lightweight machine pistol with a folding stock.

As I stated earlier Ellis Camp was not too far from where in later years they were to make the film Born Free, which is the story based on the Adamson family. Their farm was about a twenty minute drive from where we were based and occasionally we were allowed to use their swimming pool which was in the shade under a thatched roof with open sides.

We were there one day about six of us larking about in the pool, when one of the lads pointed out a colleague had been underwater a long time. He had died or drowned, we spent some time trying to resuscitate him, even after we had lifted him into the Land Rover we continued as we travelled as fast as the roads would allow back to the Medical Centre. It was my job the next morning to send a signal to Nairobi informing them of his passing away and no doubt they informed his family.

Nanuki is about thirty miles to the north of Ellis Camp and it is where the equator passes through. There was a bar, and it is probably still there, built across the invisible line which circles the globe. The bar itself has a line gouged into the drinking surface showing where the division was, so one person could be drinking in the northern hemisphere whilst another holding their hand could be drinking in the south.

A little further on is a place called Isiolo. There is nothing there except a large round water hole in the dessert surrounded by trees, it is deep enough to swim in and it is where herds of various types of animals go for water.

On a day off from duties we had driven there in a small Morris truck similar to the one we had driven back from Mombasa in, but the Army version had four-wheel drive. The water looked clear, cool and inviting and as I said deep enough to swim in which was the purpose of the journey. But on this occasion a herd of elephants came on the scene I guess to quench their thirst in the water. We grabbed our clothes and ran back to the truck just as the big bull which was leading the group took a dislike to us. It was pawing the ground and looking very angry and was coming towards us, who were by now in the rear of the vehicle. We were begging the driver to start and get us out of there. The engine started and the bull was on the move at a trot towards us, as we started to move the driver stalled the engine. It was a near miss. Quickly we were on the move again and only just staying in front of the enraged animal. With a sigh of relief from all of us in the back, the bull turned and went back to its herd.

**

The road back from Nanuki to Ellis had a murrum surface which was not very smooth, it is also slightly down hill and very straight for about twenty odd miles until it reaches a double bend with a sharp right hand turn. We had taken a few officers into Nyeri one evening, and after waiting for them for a few hours they made the decision to stay the evening, and sent us back to the Regiment.

But instead of doing what we had been told we went for a ride to Nanuki, which is in the opposite direction and meant passing Ellis Camp. On the return we were on the straight road and seeing how fast the Land Rover would go, Ted was sitting in the left hand seat and kept going to sleep, and his door became unlatched, I put my arm around him and held the door closed. I do remember seeing the Speedo reaching seventy miles per hour which is very fast for the old version we were using.

The Army was not too pleased with me; I was in charge, when we demolished the vehicle shown on the previous page. There are three seats in the front of a Land Rover, I was in the middle one when the three of us went to sleep on the long straight downhill stretch and hit that right hand bend in the road very hard at about seventy plus miles per hour.

The vehicle, according to the report, flew 106 feet (about 32 metres) in the air before landing on its roof and coming to rest. I was thrown a little further and landed on my back in the road. When I woke up it was to the noise of gun fire, which turned out to be a Police Post a little way away trying to attract attention.

Not knowing what had happened I got up and walked around the stricken vehicle thinking we could get into it and drive back to camp. When I saw it on its roof and the other two were lying in the roadway − I was not sure if they were alive or not. I suddenly felt very tired and lay down again and went to sleep. The next I knew I was being stretchered out of the back of an ambulance at the Army Hospital in Nairobi, which is about one hundred and ten miles away and I did not remember the journey. My only problem was severe bruising to my back; the other two each had a broken leg.

After holding a court of enquiry around the hospital beds, the Army forgave us for some reason, although we were fined a few shillings which was deducted out of our pay. It is difficult to understand our relief. We were expecting to be Court Marshalled as we were not on the road which we should have been following. A C.M. would have had the power to send us back to the UK. to serve time in the notorious Army Prison in Colchester.

**

I was the C.O.'s (Commanding Officer, the big boss of the Regiment himself) radio operator and travelled everywhere with him. Perhaps that had something to do with it − nothing about the accident was ever said. He had a little pet monkey which sometimes I had to look after if his batman was not

137

available. We did not get on very well and the little 'B' would bite me. I do not know what breed he was, but he was very little and would leap around the office and every so often attack me, but I suppose it was its idea of playing.

The Colonel was responsible for surveying where the Security Forces required roads. He, myself and four other men with two Land Rovers, would spend days in the wild. In the evening we would make camp, barbecue wild game we had caught and sleep on the ground beside or under the vehicles.

In those days Kenya was still part of the British Empire, and the Army was used extensively for items like road building. To the north of the country it was barren; there was very little population; the few that lived there resided in tiny hamlets in groups of mud huts normally constructed in a circular pattern with a fire burning in the centre of the compound. The occupants wore rags for clothing not leaving much to the imagination.

These people were living as their forefathers had for many centuries; there was no running water or sanitary facilities so the smell was not very pleasant around these communities. They sustained their living by either catching wildlife for their food or growing plants in the dry African earth. Each tiny community would also have a few goats or something similar. After a period when the small group of huts had served their purpose and were no longer of any use, they moved to another virgin piece of ground in this vast wilderness and built another group of dwellings.

The authorities wanted to make use of the many hundreds of square miles of almost empty land, populated by wild animals and as stated, a few small hamlets, to that end they needed to understand the terrain.

There was also the need, nearer to Nairobi where the Mau Mau had established themselves, to locate the disused tracks in the forest which were not marked on maps. Before the emergency they would have led to smallholdings, however now they had been abandoned when the terrorists started their murderous ways.

The picture on the following page was taken near Isiolo, as I stated earlier it is a well-known area because of the large watering hole, similar to a large pond, where wild animals come to quench their thirst. It is in the North of Kenya, near to the start of the Sahara Desert, although locally it is called Chalbi Desert.

At that time there were no roads and we had been travelling all day through the bush. The Land Rovers, had despite some difficult gullies and rough ground, always overcome the terrain, sometimes with a little help from ourselves. No roads only a compass and a map, it was a long time before anyone thought of Satellite Navigation.

My one regret is I do not remember my travelling companions' names. In the picture the guy on the left was the Colonel's driver, I am on the right. The fellow next to me drove the other vehicle, the last one rode shot gun with the other soldier who is taking the picture.

The only way to communicate with base was by rigging up an aerial like a washing line with RHQ in the distance on the long side of the wire, communication was by Morse code.

In the text I have used the word surveying, I do not mean in the sense of a team undertaking a full survey using theodolites and other measuring devices. We or at least the C.O. was drawing lines on a map as possible routes.

On one of our forays in the Aberdare Mountains, we were following an old unused track that was not marked on the maps. It twisted down the side of a hill the undergrowth brushing close to the vehicles as it narrowed into little more than a path. At the bottom of the hill there was a small wooden bridge which was well past its sell by date.

We spent some time reinforcing it with local material, and then lightened the loads in the Land Rovers by carrying the stores across manually. With a sigh of relief they were slowly driven to the other side and the ancient structure held.

In the picture it is possible to see a soldier kneeling in front of the Land Rover. He is clearing the radiator of brush that is jammed amongst the grill causing the vehicle to overheat − the result of driving through an overgrown path.

On another occasion, as I remember it was in the same area as the bridge. We were travelling along a dirt track when we recognised the smell of death. Before we reached it we could see the headless body lying to the side of the road. There was nothing we could do. As we passed the poor soul, the road went round a bend. There were bushes and trees on our right and behind them we came across a destroyed farmhouse. A large double storey not very old building, had been trashed by the terrorists, the dead still lying where they had been killed. Again there was nothing we could do except advise the Kenya Police. Afterwards we drove on in silence more aware of what the Mau Mau was capable of.

At that time, as already stated, there was very little improvement in the north of Kenya. Looking on Google Maps now, roads, also game parks have been developed in that area. I would like to think that some of that development, especially the main roads were the result of the days we spent in the wilderness plotting routes.

In September 1955 it was all change at the top and the Colonel was promoted and returned to London to a position in the War Office. He was replaced by another of the same rank, who like all new brooms changed things and one of those changes was me. I was transferred to Company 'D' and from there into the wilds where one of the troops were building roads. He could not have made it more obvious that I was not needed transferring me from HQ company to Four company and troop Four.

When all this happened it was the Rainy Season where week after week water falls out of the sky in a continuous downpour. Each troop had a weekly delivery of stores and I was to be taken out to the wilds in the three ton Bedford truck which was doing the run that day. As the senior person on the vehicle I sat up front next to the driver. The journey was into the Aberdare Mountains and at one point the road followed an escarpment with a steep drop into the valley on the right, as we climbed the road was covered in thick slippery mud. Despite the four-wheel drive on the lorry it slipped into the grassy wet bank on the left, the driver kept going dragging the side of the truck along this high verge and trying to get the vehicle back on the road by holding the steering hard over to the right. Suddenly the four wheels found a grip and the lorry shot across the road and one front wheel went over the edge. The more he tried to get it back on the road the further we went over the edge, because there was no grip for the tyres to respond to the steering.

The Bedford Army version was well equipped for this type of work with an electric winch to the front which could also be used to the rear of the vehicle, where there was a useful tree. We threaded the steel cable around the various pulleys and hooked it to the tree and gently wound it back to the drum. All that happened was the front of the truck swung further over the drop. Plan two was to bring the winch back to the front and take it about twenty yards further up the hill where there was another tree growing out of the bank.

Once again we started to pull the cable back to its home on the drum. It started to work the cable tightened, the lorry started to move in the right direction, then it all came to a stop when the tree came out of the ground. We were now in a hopeless situation: cold and very wet, with the two offside wheels hanging over the edge. The vehicle looked very precarious and it would not take a great deal, something like a high wind to send it over. (The film The 'Italian Job' springs to mind!)

Down in the valley we could see what looked like a large house and there was a single light showing. So I left the driver and two other sappers we were transporting, to look after the vehicle, and I would go and see if we could get some assistance. On leaving the road, the first part was very steep and I slid down the bank until it levelled out. After which it was still downhill and near to vertical and I was half running and sliding down to the level ground near the property. A large open area to the front and a building towering over it, and set in the front two large wooden doors, it was like something out of Dracula.

There were two huge circular iron door knockers, which I lifted and let them drop to attract attention. At first they only made an echoing banging sound inside the building. I stood there waiting, a soaking wet mud stained individual, not knowing what to expect and half wondering if the place was deserted. My brain started whirring trying to think of what to do next. It was a very long walk to anywhere else where there might be any form of help. After a few more knocks I could hear footsteps and then the drawing of bolts and finally the door opened a few inches, and portrayed in the gap was the face of a Nun framed in a habit.

I was allowed in but no further than the vast hall and luckily they did have a telephone which I was allowed to use. After going through various exchanges operated by personnel, I was finally put through to the duty officer at Ellis camp.

Two Land Rovers and a team of men were dispatched to us along with recovery equipment. They brought with them long stakes that were hammered into the road in a line and the winch attached to them by weaving it in and out. To the rear a rope was attached to the original tree to help stop the lorry going any further over the edge. But the most beautiful thing that they brought was hot soup – it was in a can with a fuse down the centre, one opened the can, lit the fuse and hey presto! A hot mushroom drink in a minute.

Living out in the Troops was not only boring but cold and wet. Boring because I had to stay in camp all day nursing the signal system for the troop and there was only a couple of messages a day. The others left in the morning to carry out engineering works. Every few weeks we would strike camp and move to another location as the part of road they were building moved further and further away from the living area. All very uncomfortable as it was the time of year when the rains continued, everything was soaking wet and cold. At least I did not spend anything because there were no shops and therefore nothing to buy.

After two years my days in Kenya came to an end very suddenly. The regiment was instructed to dismantle the camp and we left for Mombasa, in a very short period of time in order to catch the Captain Cook home. During the two years I was there, some men, their Army time finished, found work and stayed. I think maybe if I had got de-mobbed in East Africa I would have done the same. Although the last three months living out in the troops did put me off staying in the

Army as I was well aware I had been very lucky so far with my time and postings in the mob (Army).

*A little help for a Land Rover, because of the weight in the rear, the four-wheel drive to the front pair of wheels would not grip in the mud, my extra few pounds helped. In the background are the remains of an old African settlement.*

# Back to the Army

The Army was not going to let me go that easy. When I received my demob papers they also sent a book of Post Office vouchers, due to be paid once a month for my reserve pay. I was probably told about the reserve bit when I first joined but three years had now passed and I had forgotten about it. I now looked on it as a bonus paid to me every few weeks, not a commitment. It was 1956, time to get on with my life, but the Army had been paying me as a reservist and they wanted me to work for it.

Leaving the Army is like leaving a friend who has looked after you, paid you, provided food and a bed and generally cared for your well-being. Whilst in the mob I had met a lot of fellows who had been demobbed only to re-join and now I could understand why. Leaving is a big step; one has to find your own way in life, money, food and somewhere to live. Prisoners who are let out of jail must find it tempting to mug an old lady and steal from her so that they can be sent back to a place where they do not have to think for themselves, where everything is supplied for them. I digress.

Shortly after leaving the forces I was offered a day's interview to become a civil servant, as a result of my experience and what I had achieved in communications and my speed, not only sending but also reading Morse code. My guess it was to be at the spy centre in Cheltenham. This was no ordinary job as I was not given details of where it was or salary. Tickets for the train fare to Loughborough were attached where the interview was to be held, and I arrived on a cold and wet early morning on the specified date.

The interview was intense, not only about my family but it included a test of my skills including spelling. Spelling has never been my good point and when they asked me to spell 'character' and I started it with a 'K', I think that was when it ended and I was on my way home. On the other hand, it could have been because my father was a shop steward in a Union, which in itself would have been enough to turn me down. Father worked as a projectionist for Odeon Cinemas and he found me work at another theatre doing the same thing.

At that time trying to find work of any sort was difficult. A lot of men were leaving the Army after completing their National Service all of which would be in their twenties and most companies who wanted new recruits were looking for school leavers. At the time after chasing around looking for work, I almost wished I had stayed with Plessey.

**

I was working at the Odeon in Whalebone Lane. It was very close to the junction of Green Lanes and nearby was the Chequers Pub which was well known across the area. Almost daily new Ford cars would pass by going to the various dealerships, and from the balcony next to the operating room in the cinema we could watch them go feeling a little envious at these shiny vehicles, especially when I got on my motorbike to go home.

I had applied for a provisional license to drive the little motorbike, an Excelsior Talisman Twin, which I had bought after I had left the Army, a lively little machine in a gold colour. With my wages from the cinema, and my Army reserve pay amounting to a few shillings I could pay my way but I was not making a fortune. When the story about Egypt and Nasser, its new ruler was on the news, I did not take a lot of notice, but as I said I had taken the Queen's shilling and they wanted me to work for it.

Anthony Eden who was the Prime Minister in the fifties, he and the French Government with the help of Israel declared war on Egypt, because the Egyptians had nationalized the Suez Canal. Yes – that's right the same Canal I had sailed through earlier in the year. The waterway had been built by England and France and opened in 1869 on a 99 year lease from the Egyptian Government. So with only thirteen years to go on that lease we were at war.

The call up papers came and I was off to the Army again back to a very familiar Barton Stacey in Hampshire, from where I had been demobbed a few months earlier. It was a beautiful summer's day in August when I got off the back of the lorry that had brought a crowd of us from the station. Colonel Frank Baker, in full uniform helped me down, what an impression that was for the other fellows!

Frank shook my hand and we stood by the lorry chatting and then he invited me to go with him to the Officers Mess where he signed me in as a guest. I was in civilian clothes which was acceptable to the rules, and as a guest precluded me from buying drinks at what was a well-stocked bar.

When I finally got to the barrack room after a few drinks and very much the worst for wear, I did not let on that Frank was my brother-in-law, married to my sister Fran. He was in the Medical Corp, but how he knew I was arriving at that time I do not know, and he would not say. The other fellows in the hut, which was to be our home until the Army knew what to do with us, were curious of why a full blown Colonel should meet me off the transport and take me for a drink but they never did find out.

We only spent a little time in England, it could not have been more than a week, I do not remember. All that time the newspapers were full of the war. Would there be one? When would it start? But no firm news either way.

On parade one morning we were told we were going to Germany the next day. The following morning it was an early start standing on the parade ground in full kit and a duffle bag over your shoulder. The train was similar to the one that took the troop I was with at that time to Stansted but this time the seats had a cushion on them. When it finally reached Harwich on the East Coast it was a long walk from the train through the docks on a very wet early evening. A little out of breath we finally reached what to my eyes was a funny looking little ship, but it turned out there was nothing funny about it.

This little ship – I had seen bigger tugs in the docks in London – was to take us to the Hook of Holland and when I saw all the men lined up to go on her I wondered where they were all going to fit. And then I found out. On board below deck there was this large area with rows of bunks stacked on top of one another. The bottom one was close to the floor, the next one about nine inches above it and so on until there were about six in the tier. To get in – the top one was lifted up, then the one below until the bottom one was in view, I do not remember how the order for sleeping was, but one of us got in the bottom, then the bunk above was lowered and the next person got in and so forth to the top which was only a few inches away from the ceiling. I chickened out and went on deck because I could see the problem if the man on the bottom needed to visit the loos, which were disgusting and filthy, then everyone above would have to get up and wait until he came back. I made myself comfortable on deck which was to be a very rough crossing with the little boat being tossed around. On one of my trips below I discovered a lot of my fellow travellers could not cope with the vessel heaving and tossing and the floor was covered in their discomfort.

When we left England we had walked in our own time through the docks to the ship, the Army was not having any of that in Holland. We had to line up in three ranks and march through the streets to the railway station. The train we boarded was no comparison with the train that took us to Harwich. It was smooth when travelling along the rail lines, and inside it had comfortable seats and it whisked us on to Osnabruck in what was West Germany.

We were taken from the station in yet more Army Lorries and entered through imposing gates into an enormous barracks with a huge parade ground to the fore. We learned they were built for and used by the German S.S. during the Second World War. The building was on three floors with a flight of wide steps leading up to it. Inside the rooms were large with only four men to each and to keep the cold out the windows were triple glazed, all very comfortable − nothing like we soldiers were used to. In the cellars there were rows of cells, the British Army used them for storage but one does not want to think what their previous use was.

There were to be two Regiments of Royal Engineers at this location. The next morning we all lined up on the enormous parade ground in single file, possibly nearly a thousand men, I saw a few familiar faces but no one I knew from Kenya. At the front of the line there was a row of tables with officers sitting behind them. As we filed down they checked our documents and asked various questions, one of which was do you have a driving licence?

At that time I had a provisional license to drive the small motorbike I had bought on my demob, so I answered yes. He asked if he could see it and I told the truth by saying that I had left it at home. He ticked a box on the form but I was not to know what it meant. I moved on to the next table for more questions and then on to the end of the line, where I was sent in one direction and the lads each side of me were sent in another. It turned out that was the Army's way of forming two separate units, a single line with every other man going to a different Regiment.

The next day, and to my surprise I was allocated a FFW, (*Fitted For Wireless*) it was an Austin two ton vehicle with an office on the rear with lots of radio and electrical equipment. Although I had on occasions driven Land Rovers, when I had the opportunity whilst in Kenya, I needed to learn quickly how to control this truck.

Time dragged on and no war started, and because everything was packed awaiting instant orders for embarkation to the Middle East, the soldiers did not have many things to do. The Army really did not know what to do with all the reservists they had in Germany. On two occasions in the following three months they sent us home to the UK on leave for a long weekend. I don't think everyone returned, and went AWOL instead.

Another way of keeping us busy was to play Army games, we would drive out in convoy and go to woodlands for manoeuvres. On these events I was normally the lead vehicle with perhaps twenty or so trucks and jeeps behind me. Sitting in the cab with me was my colleague who was to help in operating the communication in the vehicle and map reading whilst on the move. The road twisted with gentle bends and then we came to the straight and were confronted by a fork in the middle of which was a petrol filling station. There was a rustle of paper beside me as my friend tried to find out where we were. Thoughts of training in Gillingham came to mind and I knew how he felt. I was asking him "Which way?" and he said after a pause "Go right." As we were on the right hand side of the road as everybody else on the Continent drive, I started to go past the fuel station when I was told by my mate that it was the other road we wanted.

The ribbing that went on in the NAAFI (*Canteen*) afterwards was merciless. Although we were too late for the road junction, I had turned left and driven through the forecourt, past the petrol pumps, with the pump attendant standing next to them looking in wonderment. We continued through the forecourt and out the other side onto the road we should have been on. Looking in the driving mirrors I saw all the other vehicles doing the same.

One evening we were given permission to go into the local town. A group of us were walking along a street when suddenly there was a siren and a flashing blue light. It was a police car which came around a bend and was creating the noise and lights. I was fascinated because in England emergency vehicles had bells on the front and did not have flashing lights, not at that time anyway.

It was in December. When we woke up in the morning to discover the other Regiment had left, and it was they who landed in Egypt to clear the way for the following invasion. A little time after, while waiting to go out and join them, we were sent home for Christmas. But instead of joining them and a trip to Egypt the war came to an end and once more I was demobbed, but this time I had a driving licence without taking a test.

Enough of the Army, let's get back to leaving it and wondering what to do with myself.

**

A near miss with a car which turned in front of me at a cross roads made a difference to my life. To avoid it I had to swerve the Excelsior Motorbike around the front of the vehicle to miss it, which frightened me very much and I was shaking. In that instant my mind was changed about motorbikes and I started looking for a car.

To fund my living I took a job with London Transport as a conductor on the buses, which was in the days when they used to have a driver and a person to collect the passengers' fares. The journey every day was on the number 8 bus, which went from Old Ford in East London to Neasden in North London en route passing through Oxford Street. We did the journey twice a day although on occasions when it was the rush hour we detoured to London Bridge Station in South London. One day I changed the board on the front of the bus to say we were going to London Bridge but my driver out of habit did not take the turn for the station and continued as if we were going to our normal destination. There was panic inside the vehicle as passengers realised they were going the wrong way, funny nobody really complained but just got off to complete their journey. But the funny thing after that was the driver realised he had gone wrong and to get to the station he took the bus down small narrow side streets, much to the people on the pavements amazement.

After about six months I was bored and started looking for something else to do and seriously thinking of going back in the Army. This feeling had followed another instance when I was very late one morning and three buses had gone out in front of us. So to make up time I would not let the driver stop until we had passed the other two in front of us. It was lovely seeing the look on people's faces as we roared past and even funnier when we caught up with the others and passed them as well.

Out with the lads one evening I was told there was a driving vacancy in Dagenham at Toleman and Wright. It was a company with a contract for keeping the production lines at Fords clear by taking completed cars as they came off the line, driving them to a parking area, from there they would be taken to their allocated destinations.

There were three separate groups of line drivers so as to give 24 hour coverage to keep the end of the production line clear. The job was to take all types of vehicles to a holding park, and on odd occasions move them by road, either to the docks or to Ford dealerships around the country. There were regular drivers who did this work, but when they were short-handed we, that is the line drivers, would be allocated a vehicle to deliver to a dock or other destination. On one occasion I delivered a police car to somewhere in the Midlands and I had also been to Liverpool docks. In those days car transporters were just starting to be developed, so most deliveries were by road.

Shortly after the instance at the cross roads with the Excelsior Talisman twin, I took my own advice and changed the motorbike for an Austin 10 Cambridge 1938 model, registration DKC134.

The car had a top speed of about 55 MPH, no power searing and with rod brakes, which meant the system was operated by a series of steel rods with a linking arrangement to the four wheels. Pressing the pedal meant anything could happen; sometimes the car would pull to the right other times to the left, rarely straight ahead. One tended not to rely on braking and used the gearbox to slow and to control the speed of the car. The cars we were taking off the line at Fords like all modern cars had hydraulic systems – what a difference.

For a long time after the war most vehicles that were being produced went for export. In order to buy a new car in the UK involved a waiting list, two years or longer was not unusual. Most cars on the road were pre-war, so my Austin was not out of place.

I had been at the firm for about a year, when what had started as a normal day driving finished products or other vehicles off the production lines, parking them in a large pound in rows of model and colour. This was great training for driving as every car was different, left-hand drive – right-hand drive, big or small, manual or automatic, the occasional articulated truck and sometimes coaches.

It was a bright sunny day when I got back into the yard from the line; I was called to the office and asked if I would take a car to Bristol Docks. I jumped at the chance, it was better pay and broke the monotony of going back and forth to the plant with different vehicles.

It was also in this period that I would frequently go to the Ford jetty; a lot of the cars destined for the Continent were exported from there. This was the same jetty that as a child I had been shipped from to be saved from the German bombers.

The car was a basic left-hand drive two door beige Anglia 100E quite a lively little thing – entirely opposite from my lumbering old Austin. Before leaving I was told the car had to be in Bristol by three that afternoon to catch the ship on which it was to be exported, not leaving a lot of time for the journey. Normally vehicles were sent days before they were to be exported.

The M4 motorway out of London to the West had only been completed in some places and for most of the journey it was a case of taking the very busy A4 which was classed as a single road with a lane in each direction, plus the occasional centre lane which was used for passing.

Just outside Maidenhead to the west of London, there was a long queue of single line traffic wending its way towards a roundabout; the centre lane was empty so I used that. A little way along I saw a two tone coloured beige Bentley pull out of the line and start to follow, at first I thought he was in a hurry and had twigged he could use the centre lane.

He started flashing his lights and I assumed I was in the way and he wanted to pass. As I got to the roundabout I thought if I go right round I would be out of his way and he could go whatever way he wanted. He followed me. I resumed driving on the A4 towards Bristol. He was now close to the boot of the little car flashing his lights. If he was asking me to stop it was not possible as to do so would have brought the other traffic to a standstill as the road was solid with vehicles and there was nowhere to park.

After a little while there were two lorries moving along at about 25–30 MPH with a gap between them. I could see a lay-by coming up so I swept the diminutive 100E in between the moving space of the two goods vehicles. The little car responded beautifully, and I pulled up in the parking area, leaving the Bentley with nowhere to go but straight ahead as the second lorry trundled past. I was worried I was thinking that maybe it was somebody wanting to steal the unregistered car I was driving.

I got out of the car and stood in the sun giving the other car plenty of time to get out of my way. To my astonishment he came back, went round the roundabout and pulled up behind me. He was a white-haired, elderly gentleman, with a white clipped moustache and a well-dressed, young, blonde woman in the front seat of his car.

'What is your name?' was his greeting. I was on the brink of losing my temper; I thought '*what the hell was wrong with this guy.*' I looked him straight in the eye and without raising my voice answered something like 'King Alfred.' This wasn't very clever, as I had antagonised him even more. He was also probably feeling a little foolish in front of his lady friend. It turned out he was a close friend of the Chairman of the English Ford Motor Company and was on his way to have lunch with him.

It was about ten days later that Toleman and Wrights were told if they wanted to keep their contract with Fords, I had to go. So after thirteen months I was out of a job again. In those days unions were not very powerful, anyway I was not a member, but my guess is if the same situation happened today then shop stewards would call everyone out on strike, member or no member.

In Chadwell Heath High Road, there was a small car sales site selling second hand cars. I went in to see if they had any work, the owner asked me if I could zero the speedo readings on the cars, I had seen Dad do it when he sold the big seven, so I said yes and he offered me a sum of money for each one I did. To turn the speedometers back to zero this meant taking the dashboard out releasing the cable from the instrument taking the back off it to get at the numbers and then turning the milometer back. As I remember there was a silver-coloured Sunbeam Talbot, a beautiful car which was the only vehicle I could not achieve my work on. After a while I progressed to selling cars. Today this work of tampering with milometers is unlawful and banned, but in the fifties it was common practice. The argument being the company selling the car could not guarantee the mileage and it was more honest to turn them back.

Father was not too pleased and carried on about when I was going to earn a proper living and pay my way. One day that all came to a head so I moved out. It was the period when the secondhand car sales were very strong, few people owned cars and everyone wanted one. Car sites were busy places especially over the weekends.

I had a need to live somewhere in a time when any form of accommodation was scarce, this was a result of the millions of houses that had been destroyed in the war. A friend had a car site called 'East Anglia Car Sales' which was situated on a plot of land and a very old wooden barn in Rectory Road, Pitsea, Essex, with an unused caravan behind it. I moved into the ancient van and sold cars from the small frontage. Some of the cars were old, ten or more years. We also sold ex post office vans which we had repaired and sprayed in the barn. It was the American cars that caused the most interest.

The caravan was a bit lopsided, I did level it out before moving in, but it had to go not only was it too small but very basic and with little insulation so the inside could get very cold. The brand new one which replaced it was twenty-two feet long (about seven metres) which was very comfortable. On the occasions we had a party, there was enough room for about ten or twelve people to enjoy themselves.

In the evenings, there was quite a lot to do. There were various cinemas, about three in all, showing different films. It was very rare that we went into pubs; coffee bars were more likely where we would meet.

I, with others, became a regular visitor and then a member of The Shandon Dance Club in Romford, which was about the only regular dancing facility and you had to be a member by law to be able to go in. The music was a mixture of modern, jazz and country. The favourites were the Irish reels. As I remember one of which was the Waltz of Limerick where you went round and round with your partner, getting faster and faster.

On one of my visits to the Shandon, I met Tony Goffin. We used to see each other from time to time mainly at weekends; he lived at the other end of East Road in Adelaide Gardens. Tony was a commercial traveller for Bex Bissell touring the country selling cleaning tools to shops and stores, which meant he was away week days returning on Fridays.

I feel sorry for youngsters today looking for a career; it was so easy in the fifties to find work or to be self-employed. For instance at one period I sold ice cream from a van, very good money, all I needed to be able to do the work was a driving license. Hygiene certificates probably existed but were not heard of which no doubt you would need today. If you wanted to set up a window cleaning round to earn a few bob then you did. I never did but I know a few people who found a living that way. If they used a ladder or other device, it was their problem for their own security – they were not bothered by Health and Safety. They also earned good money.

It seems at the time of writing, everything in the UK is governed by red tape, licences, safety at work, certificates of training and a host of other pieces of paper to be able to find employment. No wonder the country has problems – well it has at the time of writing.

I do not remember there being any pattern to it, but we, that is my brother and I, who had moved into the caravan with me after he left the Army, would hold a party in the van and Tony, would sometimes have a party at his parents' house. As I say there was no pattern to it, just the opportunity to get together socially.

My friendship with Tony was a bit strange in that he worked away all week and I worked on Saturdays. I had been working late in Pitsea, and it was party night at Tony's about twenty miles away. I was delayed because I was selling a car to a customer, and by time the deal was done the party would have started and would have been underway for sometime also it would take about forty minutes to get there. I had been debating with myself whether to go or not. Finally I got changed, and made the effort to drive to Chadwell Heath, feeling very tired after a long day. I turned into Tony's road.

As I got out of the car I could hear music coming from the house. I walked up the path to the front door wondering why I had bothered to come. Pressing the door bell, chimes could be heard from somewhere inside. I was standing there humming to the sound of the music trying to get into the mood, when I heard high heel footsteps approaching. The door opened. I caught my breath. A vision in a beautiful light blue dress with a tight bodice and a flared skirt appeared. My heart did a flip even before this beautiful lady looked into my eyes with a lovely smile and said, "You must be Percy?" I knew then this was the lady I wanted to spend my life with.

I do not remember my reply, I was too stunned to speak, and I followed her through the passage into the front room of the house. What a terrible disappointment when Tony introduced Jean to me as his new girlfriend.

The evening drifted past, music playing and a lot of laughter. Most of the time Jean was talking to Tony and some other friends, but occasionally she would look my way and smile. I was feeling sorry for myself and wishing that I had given the party a miss, I left early.

# Courting

I had been courting an Irish girl for quite some time, Jo, nice lady, who was training to be a nurse at Oldchurch Hospital in Romford. It had been an on and off difficult friendship as she was a devout Catholic, which made any form of relationship, if you weren't of that religion, difficult, and although I never met her parents I understand they were not too happy.

On one occasion the four of us, that is Tony, Jean, Jo and I, went to Clacton in Essex for a day out. It was a pleasant enough day, a bit overcast and it was a beautiful ride in a Humber Hawk, but for some reason it was not the fun day it should have been. Perhaps it was because of the invisible pull between Tony's female friend and me.

At one time to please Jo, I tried to convert to her religion, but it was something I could not get on with, I also found the Priest dominating, which made my hairs stand on end, and after escaping from my own father's clutches, that was not something I wanted. When I gave up trying to change my religion, it was at a time when Jo was going to Lourdes in France to worship at the Basilica. I had arranged to collect her at a train terminal in London. But she never arrived and I never saw her or heard from her again.

If you are sincere, but honestly want to impress a lady then you turn up in something like the picture below: An American, two year old, 19 foot (six metres) long Oldsmobile 98 Rocket.

The one I arrived at Jean's parent's house was in a lilac colour. It had central locking with electric windows, self-searching radio, air conditioning, power steering, automatic gearbox and white leather seats. It also had a white soft top − a press of a button and the roof disappeared into the boot. It was totally smooth and quiet as it glided along. Nothing new in those toys in today's cars but the mass produced British cars at that time did not have anything like these items.

It had been a few weeks after the party. Jo was in France and I also knew Tony was away when I telephoned Jean, at Lloyd's Bank in Romford, where she worked, asking to take her out. To my joy Jean agreed. I collected her that evening from her parents' home, and we drove up to the West End of London.

I don't think her mother and father were impressed, I had black wavy hair, I lived in a caravan and drove around in various cars, with respect to the travelling people, they thought I was a gypsy. I was probably a very poor second to the debonair commercial traveller Tony, to start dating their daughter.

The barn and the sales site were closed down by the local council, as they argued 'it was not fit for purpose'. Charlie who owned the site had been trying to obtain planning approval for car sales and repairs, but it was not forthcoming. The local authority insisted that a beautiful old building should be preserved and not be used as a vehicle workshop and a car sales site. They were probably right.

I did not need a certificate, there was no such thing, just a history in sales when I started looking for work again. I finally landed a job with Reeves Garage in Chadwell Heath, a firm that had been established for over thirty years. The company that owned it had other branches in London. Reeves were on the Romford Road on the edge of town in a lovely thirties building that has now gone forever. For convenience I moved back home to Mill Lane, Chadwell Heath; a house my parents had moved to from East Road whilst I was in the Army.

The job turned out to be disappointing. The deal was a basic salary and commission for every vehicle I sold. It sounded good; with a demand for new vehicles very high it seemed perfect. The reality was very different as there was an up to two year's waiting list for a new car. I would take a deposit and the balance was due when the car was ready for delivery, which meant I did not get my commission until that time. Reeves did not sell secondhand cars. Those vehicles went elsewhere so there was no commission to be earned that way. The job was not what I expected. Of course, the company had the same problem in that it was not making any money either, until delivery of the vehicles that were on order from the factory.

Renault Motors in France started producing the Dauphine, with an engine at the rear. The cars were readily available and the firm I worked for started to import them. A poor replacement to the English cars we had on offer, but it was small and nippy and once you got used to a floppy gear lever, which did not seem to know which gear it was in, it was quite fun to drive, and it was new.

On most days I would use one of the Renaults to pick Jean up for lunch, collecting her outside the bank we would go and have egg and chips or something similar sitting outside a café on the edge of town. Tony did not seem to mind the arrangements. On a visit to me at Reeves, while I was busy, he was talking to the girl who worked in the office, Barbara. He eventually started seeing a lot of her, and in due course, married her.

I was offered work at the Richmond Motor Co at the bottom of Richmond Hill, West London. They sold Austin and Morris cars. It was at the time when the new Austin Mini Van was being introduced. After a desperate search I finally found somewhere to live − it was a dirty and scruffy room on the fourth floor, overlooking the entrance to Kew Gardens. The bathroom and the toilet were on the floor below down a joint staircase shared with others who also rented rooms. The electrics were very poor and low powered for it took two hours to boil an egg on the small electric stove in the room.

On the ground floor there was a telephone with a coin box which took two one penny pieces, Jean and I would talk for hours while I fed the box every few minutes with two pence pieces. Some evenings I would drive over and see her. There were thirty sets of traffic lights at that time between Richmond and Chadwell Heath. If I caught all of them at red then it would take an hour and a quarter, if they were all at green − thirty-five minutes.

In September 1960, when Jean was twenty and I was nearly twenty-five we got engaged and the wedding was arranged for the following March. Everybody said it would not last. Fifty plus years later, at the time of writing, I think we got it right!

**

Godfrey Davis in the sixties was a very large and well-known car hire organisation and also the seller of new Ford cars in Neasden, North London, which is not too far from Wembley Stadium. Their huge property fronted onto the main road. In one part a large showroom where new cars were sold. The remainder of the property was where they retailed second hand vehicles which had been refurbished from their hire fleet – they also turned the milometers back to zero. Some of the cars were disposed of to the trade but others were retailed from the forecourt.

G.D had run an advert in the Auto Trader for car sales people, which I answered and was invited to go for an interview with their sales director. At the interview I made it clear that I was getting married the following March, and my fiancée would be allowed an extra week's break for her honeymoon from Lloyd's Bank, and a further normal fortnight's holiday which was the bank's attitude to newlyweds. I asked for the same provision, which was agreed, providing I was not paid for one of the weeks. There was no written contract the director made notes on his sheet, I thought no more about it thinking it had been accepted. In the meantime the bank transferred Jean to a local branch.

We were desperate to find somewhere to live. We toured around North London, answering adverts of 'properties to let' in the newspapers. The places we looked at were just scruffy rooms, very few had their own bathroom or kitchen, we were getting very depressed spending days looking at rubbish.

With the exception of Aunt Monica, Mum's sister who was a Nun, the rest of her close family I'd only heard of by name. I had never met George Fanning, her Catholic brother-in-law, the owner of a large building company in Mill Hill; it was with some surprise when we learned he had offered us a first floor maisonette (A flat with its own front door to the street) not too far from the town centre.

Our worries were over. Another surprise there was no key money required; just a month's rent in advance. He did not say but we were sure the property was owned by George and as the rent was paid to an agent we had no knowledge who owned it.

Godfrey Davis was all I expected. When I first started I was assigned to selling new cars. It was the period just after the new 105E Anglia came on the market which had a rear window that sloped forward at the lower edge. There was healthy interest in the car and unlike the other makes I had been selling, there was immediate delivery on some models.

On one occasion a tall man in a turban came in to the showroom with his family and bought a white 105E which he collected a few days later. I explained to him it had a one year guarantee and if anything was to go wrong with it please get in touch. A few days later there was a telephone call for me, it was my Turban friend. 'Mr Chattey, the car has come to a stop.' I was thinking of organising the breakdown wagon to go to his aid, when he said the dial on the dashboard with a little petrol pump on it, the needle has gone to E. I said it needs petrol, he wanted to know how we got petrol to him − it turned out he thought the guarantee covered refuelling as well, he was very disappointed when I finally made him realise it did not.

Left over from my Pitsea days was a guy who owed me a substantial sum of money. His wife was a seamstress so in lieu of payment she supplied the material and made Jean's wedding dress. We went a few times to Basildon where they lived, I would go and get lost so that they could get on with the design and make the garment.

Back to Godfrey Davis and before the great day arrived, I had been transferred to the used car section. My personal allocated car that I had been using not only for business but also for pleasure was taken from me. The used car team were allowed to use one of the second hand vehicles that were for sale, to go home in or even on holiday. Of all the beautiful cars that were available for me to go to my wedding and honeymoon, was not to be. The sales manager thought it very funny when he allocated an old Ford Popular that we had taken in part exchange that morning. I had had a funny feeling when I saw it arrive, that that was going to happen.

The Popular of 1946 vintage was a pig to drive. With its transfer suspension it would roll alarmingly on corners, it had a three speed gearbox and was about as fast as two people on a tandem. With two small, hard, uncomfortable bucket seats in the front, no heater or radio, it sort of trundled along with a load of noise. But I smiled and took it. He's probably still laughing.

It was a beautiful sunny day in March. After a few drinks down the pub with Dad and my brother Bob, we went back to Mill Lane to get changed. Dad had had too much to drink and collapsed on his bed and did not move. We tried to wake him but it was not possible. That was a problem; he was supposed to be picking up Nan and Granddad, who lived about two miles away, also along with Aunt Mag and another guest who had come up from Brighton for the wedding and was staying with them.

The two door Ford Popular did sterling work that afternoon. With only four seats and a suspension fit for a rock and roll roundabout, we got six in it, albeit it meant my brother standing with his feet on the internal floor boards and hanging on to the open door. I was late, well late. I should have been in the church settling the fee with the vicar; instead I was collecting guests and parking the car.

What I did not know was that while I was rushing around they were trying to delay Jean. One of our friends was the driver using Jeans Dad's car, and when the bridesmaids were dropped off and I still had not arrived they delayed Jean from arriving. I am sure Jean's Dad thought I had bottled out as they drove round the block wasting time. When I finally arrived, the Reverend Marshall insisted on going into the vestry to settle the money side. Then we had another problem – he could not give me change from the five pound note I gave him, so I told him to keep the difference, he was most grateful for the tip of four pounds twelve shillings and six pence.

From then on everything went smoothly, the church looked great, it was Mothering Sunday and it was bedecked in flowers from the midday service. The wedding party held later in the scout's hut was underway, when the photographer arrived to tell us that he had used two cameras and one of them had not worked, asking if he could take the pictures again that had not come out.

The evening sped by and at last we got changed and were ready to leave in that car. Everybody stood around and we waved as we got into the jalopy. I started the engine, we smiled at each other, I put it in gear and with a puff of smoke we moved away for no more than twelve feet. There was an almighty bang and the engine sounded as if the silencer had come off. It was worse; someone had tied a thick piece of rope to the exhaust with a length of cast iron drain pipe on the end. The pipe had got hooked behind the wheels of a parked car and had pulled the whole of the exhaust system out including the part fitted to the engine. I think they meant it to make a noise like tin cans – not damage the car!

Jean's Dad, bless him, loaned us his car to go away in. The car, a Vauxhall Wyvern, was a joy to drive. Although while away I worried how I was going to explain to Godfrey Davis what had happened to their car. I had no need my uncle, Bob, who had a car repair shop did us proud by putting it back together again.

# White Cars

If you throw a dice sometimes it will be a lucky throw and roll to a stop showing the six face up, other times the one. White Cars was a lucky throw, it lasted for twelve years, and the spin off by other similar companies exists today. It came about by a series of events, each one so different from the Private Car Hire industry the result was too remote to visualise. We will go back to just after the wedding.

Number 5, Page Court in Mill Hill was a delight, totally self-contained, with two bedrooms, a large lounge and a kitchen with a built in fridge. Domestic refrigerators were very rare in those days, what more could a newly married couple require. At the rear it overlooked vast gardens with a mansion standing behind a row of trees, the estate we could look into belonged to Edmundo Ross, a famous band leader of the period.

The days drifted by, it was a beautiful spring; Jean was transferred to a branch in Mill Hill where she met film stars of the time who lived nearby − through their banking. I was content in what I was doing, the cars were good value and I sold with confidence. With George, another salesman, each month we would vie for the position of who sold the most cars. Sometimes I would sell more than five cars in a week, but other weeks it would be the reverse. Between the two of us we sold more vehicles than the rest of the seven people in the sales team.

With our joint incomes we were very comfortable. On Jean's 21st birthday we went to London's West End, to see the new stage show *Stop the World I want to get off*, starring Anthony Newley. Other times we were frequently invited to parties, the social life was good.

In September when I had been at Godfrey Davis for about nine months we both took our annual holiday, this time I was using the Ford Anglia, the one with the unique rear window. We drove to Blackpool for the first week just lazing around, visiting friends and relations back in Dagenham for the second week.

During my time with G.D, they sent me to Ford's Training School in Brentwood in Essex for a week, I think it was called Bower House. There was a unit there that bought all different makes of cars and pulled them apart to see how they were built, there was also a track to test cars on, I can remember going round it in a super charged Anglia – what a little beast that was. The course was all about product knowledge; we stayed in Ford's Hotel and spent the days comparing different makes of vehicles, sales techniques and Ford vehicles and how good they were.

We had been back about two weeks from our Annual Holiday. I was sitting in the sales office when Redfern the CEO, who was the adopted son of Godfrey Davis and had succeeded him when he had passed on earlier that year, marched into the office. A tall slim man, in an immaculate grey suit, he stood over me at my desk and he was demanding to know why I was entitled to three weeks' holiday in a year, when he only got two.

I explained that had been the agreement I had with the sales director when he had employed me so as to match my wife's entitlement from the bank. He went off saying he would ask the sales director to confirm what I had told him. He came back very quickly; I didn't think he had had time to go across the road to the offices.

He said I had lied to him and that I was to leave the site immediately. Of course, today one would have a contract and the situation could not occur. What surprised me was my wage packet and other documents had already been made up. It did seem at the time a strange reason for telling someone to leave immediately, and for Redfern to deal with it personally. I had only seen him a couple of times before and never on the sales site. Another thing I could not understand is why he would not let me confront the sales director. I could not help wondering if my history with Fords, after the Toleman and Wrights issue had caught up with me and my name had come to the fore, sliding across someone's desk at Fords after the Training School.

It was not known at that time, and possibly not now either— I certainly did not know about the offices in premises which are situated near Leicester Square in London. The function of this building is to monitor employees of large companies and it is very secret. They record members of unions names – shop stewards and the like, or troublemakers even those that had caused displeasure to a company. Their work is only known to those large firms who have been invited to join their organisation. I got to know of it when I was involved in the insurance industry – as I explain later.

It was a disaster: I was not going to get another job in sales with a history of being sacked that I now had. The only work I could find was on a commission only basis, and with Jean's money just about covering the rent on the maisonette I needed to do something quickly.

In the 1960s if you had a full driving licence you were by law allowed to drive any size vehicle, with the exception of public service vehicles, like buses or coaches. When I saw an advertisement in the newspaper 'Drivers Wanted' I applied and got the job. So I started work driving a Bedford short wheelbase tipper.

I won't dwell on the subject too long, but driving one down Petticoat Lane, London, on a market day loaded with sand is a little difficult, the stall holders were not very happy, especially if they had to move their stall to let me through.

I was allowed to take the tipper home at night, a bit different to some of the lovely cars I had arrived in when at Godfrey Davis.

In 1962 it was a bitterly cold winter. One night the tipper was loaded with fine sand, for delivery the next day, what I did not realise was that sand could freeze solid. When I tipped the back of the truck the next morning on a building site, I was busy looking down doing the paper work for the journey, I felt the wagon move and went to get out of the cab only to find the front wheels had come off the ground and had continued to rise until the truck was standing on its rear tailgate, the sand still in it. It is not very easy digging frozen sand out of the back of a tipper.

We had bought an old Austin A40 van to get around in. It was maroon and black, no heater, and seats that were worn out and very uncomfortable. It got very cold while driving, and there seemed to be freezing draughts coming from everywhere. The moisture from our breathing frosted on the inside of the windscreen so that we had to keep scraping it off as we drove along.

Things had to get better, my wages from driving was pitiful, we were cold and tired and there did not seem to be a way out. It was the Plessey Company that came to our aid, the same one I had started work with twelve years previously but not in the sense that they did anything to help. Right opposite the factory in Ley Street was a row of shops which their workers would visit to buy goods on their way to and from the factory.

It had come as a suggestion from my father, who a few years previously, with Mother, had opened a shop in Rose Lane, Chadwell Heath as a cycle and toy shop, called Chattey's and I think Dad could see the shop in Ley Street with the family name over it as a branch. Rose Lane was a new development of shops, flats and houses built on playing fields just north of the Eastern Avenue opposite the junction with East Road. At that time there were no big supermarkets or out of town stores like there are today, people shopped at their local shops, a small unit could provide a steady income.

Dad told us that there was this rundown retail outlet in Ley Street selling the same items as he was and we could have it for a song. There was also a very large flat over it which was included.

Looking back now, how we achieved it I cannot remember. There was some stock that went with the deal, so we gave notice at our home in Mill Hill, Jean left the bank and we became shopkeepers with a massive task to change a run down dirty shop into something more acceptable.

The part that stands out in my mind is the kitchen in the flat, it must have had twenty years or more of thick grease from cooking on the ceiling, and it was going to take a lot of effort to clean it.

The only heat in the three floors of the building was a coal fire in the front first floor living room. The first winter we lived there it was bitterly cold. It was the worst weather that there had been for many years and is still referred to as one of the coldest on record.

In the evening we would sit in the lounge in front of a struggling coal fire trying to give us some heat, watching a small black and white TV set in the corner, which only had two stations on it as there were no other broadcasters. Originally television only had the BBC station sending out pictures a few hours a day. It was in 1955 while I was in the Army in Kenya when commercial television started to broadcast, and only then on one station.

We would sit as close to the fire as we could with snow piled up against the window and frost on the inside of the glass. Every so often a mouse would walk across the floor, stop and look at us and disappear into the wood work. These pests, which we had inherited, were probably left over from the days when the premises was a grocers shop. We got ourselves a cat and solved that problem.

Outside the roads were very icy, not many were gritted, with snow piled up on the pavements and in the gutters. One did not dare touch the brakes when driving, the road surface was much too slippery and all control would be lost.

The other thing that makes me, and made me very happy was the love of my life Jean. She had every reason to complain but did not; she helped and got on with the situation giving me all the support that I needed. Something I will always be grateful for.

We had not been in the shop very long, when the Cold War between Communist Russia and the West flared up and started to get frightening. With the help of Cuba the Russians started to build missile bases on the island which meant the rockets could reach America including Washington, with ease. Kennedy, the then President mobilised his atomic forces and threatened to use them if the bases were not dismantled. After a few days of tension the Russians backed down.

The shop, once we had started to clean and tidy it also displaying the wares to be viewed easily, customers started to visit and very slowly we started to take money. Lunch times, when the factory people had their break meant we did good business. On display we had a good sample of cycles with various brochures for models we did not keep in stock. We could obtain most makes from wholesalers, or maybe even Dad would have the type required at the Rose Lane shop.

Besides selling cycles I used to repair them. In the rear of the premises there was a large room, which in the late 1800s when the property was built would have been the parlour where the owners would have lived. With a work bench and a clamp to hold bikes while I worked on them, it was the ideal place. I also used to buy secondhand cycles, and with others we had taken in part exchange we would sell them by lining them up on the large pavement outside the shop. The old van was useful for collecting or delivering machines.

*Our Labrador Rowdy in the shop, he loved climbing up ladders.*

After a time, my thoughts were that an old, hand painted, worn out van was not the right image for the shop. It also used a lot of oil and was expensive to run, and a pig to drive especially when it was cold. We decided to buy something different and we settled on the Ford 5cwt van which was large enough to get a couple of cycles in the rear, it also had a heater to keep your feet warm.

The only firm that would give us a decent offer for the A40, in part exchange, was Godfrey Davis, so we settled on a new bright yellow one from them.

Everything was fine and in 1963 we were expecting our first child Anne. We had a good clientele in the shop, a bright new vehicle, and if we wanted to get away for a few days my mother would look after the business.

In July Anne arrived, by coincidence on my mother's birthday the eleventh. By this time we had decorated the flat, rearranged the shop and also had a new shop front fitted to replace the old one which had 'Greens', embedded in the tiling below the glazing, which was the name of the grocer's shop (who supplied the mice) before our predecessor changed its use to cycles and toys.

Sometime before we were married the caravan I used to live in we had towed to North Devon where we installed it on a caravan site being developed at Woolacombe, called Twitchen. It was an old large house situated on the hills above the beaches, near a small hamlet called Mortehoe. For a break from the shop, my mother would open it and look after the sales so we could have a short holiday in the caravan driving down in the new little Ford. In the small village was a nice, comfortable little pub and we got to know the licensee John Green, very well, but more about him later.

In the picture is our dog Rowdy, who we got as a full grown Labrador from Battersea Dog's Home after someone had tried to break into the rear of the premises by trying to cut the glass in the workshop window. The dog soon settled down and made a noise if anybody came near when we were closed. He just loved climbing up ladders and would sit on the top for hours!

Down one side of the shop, there were cycles for sale all lined up, and to save space we had others hanging from the wood panelled ceiling. One night we had forgotten to lock the front door of our business. The local beat policeman whose job it used to be was to check doors to see if they were locked for the night. He pushed our door and it opened so he came into the shop. From the workshop, where Rowdy slept, there came a thundering noise as the large black dog chased down the passageway, with crashing sounds as he knocked over boxes of goods stored there. He then entered the shop at full speed and collided with the cycles which fell over in a domino effect. The noise frightened the life out of us asleep upstairs – I don't know how the policeman felt!

About this time a company had set up in London to rival the dominance of the traditional London black cabs. They were using my old friend, the Renault Dauphine, and calling themselves 'Minicabs'. They quickly became very successful. The only difference between them and a normal cab, besides the size of the vehicle, was people were not allowed to hail one in the street. To obtain one you telephoned a number and they would radio the nearest car to go to your address and pick you up. The story was in the news, at the time it did not bother us as we were happy with what we were doing.

At 500 miles the new van went in for its first service at the local Ford Dealer and it was discovered that the vehicle had been in a serious accident and the repair was not very professional. We took the matter up with Godfrey Davis, but they refused to talk about it and they were not prepared to do anything about it. I was livid. So we involved the AA, who inspected the vehicle at their workshop in West London after which they provided a lengthy written report detailing the damage which we sent to the Ford Motor Company. We finally got a result. It was agreed that providing we purchased a higher value vehicle from Godfrey Davis then they would credit us with what we had paid for the van.

In 1963 Ford had started producing a new model: the Cortina Estate which was an addition to their range of saloon cars. Because we needed a car that we could transfer cycles in, it suited our needs. After some discussion we agreed that we would buy one of the new vehicles part exchanging the van for it. We were given a colour chart and settled on a lime green and white one. Weeks and months went past and there was no sign of the car. I got tired of the run around and asked what they had in stock. The reply was an all-white one, so we settled on that and built a garage in the back yard to house it.

In the early fifties, first radios and then televisions were losing the valves inside the sets to make them work and being replaced by tiny transistors to receive the signals. Valves were the size of light bulbs, which took a long time to warm up before they could function and you needed about half a dozen or more in a radio set for it to operate. Plessey was in the forefront of this new technology and they were manufacturing a small portable radio that ran off a petite nine volt PP3 battery. Batteries were one of the items we sold in the shop and the people working in the factory would come across to buy them. They could purchase these very popular small radio sets at a discount from the factory. The Ever Ready van would call on us once a week to replace the stock we had sold.

One week when the salesman called we only wanted a few PP3s instead of the dozens we normally ordered, he thought it was strange, and so did we, but we did not think too much about it. Over the next few days we noticed a drop off in trade, lunch times which were normally very busy but now we saw very few customers. The people that were coming into the shop were asking for brochures with the excuse that they had not made up their mind as to what to buy. Then one day I saw a man leaving the factory with a brand new cycle still in its wrapping. I recognised him as a person who had asked for a brochure a few days earlier. It was then that we discovered that Plessey had opened a shop in the factory where their workers could buy anything at discount prices.

We were devastated as we could not compete and the shop could not pay for itself without the factory staff buying from us, as the passing trade was minimal, especially when the local council had laid no parking yellow lines outside in the road. A few weeks went by and the whole row of shops was ruined, nobody was taking enough money to make a living.

Cycles when delivered from the factory came wrapped and needed to be assembled; brakes, pedals, chains, mudguards and other items needed to be fixed to the frame. It was a bit galling when people who had bought new bikes from the factory brought them into us wanting me to assemble them.

The minicab trade in Central London was constantly in the news and from time to time one of the little red Renault Dauphines could be seen bringing a fare into Ilford. I got to thinking, we had the Cortina Estate. If we used that would the same system work locally? It was far better than the car doing nothing parked in the garage. So we started to advertise and the phone started to ring and White Cars was born.

# POB
# (Passengers on Board)

If we had spent years planning, it could not have been a better time to start a business, because of the free publicity from the national newspapers concerning the story of the Minicabs in London and how the licensed cab trade was objecting. A lot of the stories were on the front pages mostly describing how economical the minicabs were in comparison with the normal taxi.

The advertisement we put in the local press in a small box was read by people locally looking for an alternative to a taxi. By coincidence the very well established car hire company which had been operating nearby for tens of years had started to run its business down leaving us almost on our own.

The days were working out well. In the beginning, Jean would run the shop, I would sell and mend new and second hand bikes and if the phone went, for somebody needing to be taken somewhere, then I would get in the car, do the journey, and come back and carry on as normal.

It was around about this time that President Kennedy was assassinated in Dallas by being shot in the head when travelling in an open top car on a visit to the city. It was a very sad time as the man was well respected around the world; it was also a worrying time as we did not know what sort of reaction would take place.

It was not long before the car hire business started to obtain regular customers. I was doing more and more driving and the work in the shop started to get behind. After a few months there was so much use for the car that we were finding it difficult to cope, especially as we offered a 24-hour service. It became quite normal for the phone to ring, not only in the evening, but also late at night.

We needed to come to a decision. We had started this business which we thought would be part-time and some extra income to help, as the shop was not taking enough money to cover costs. But now there was too much and things were getting out of hand.

It became impossible to operate a 24-hour service with one car and one driver. At the weekends we would work 72 hours continually with Jean answering the phones and me driving, picking up a fare and taking them somewhere, and then finding a telephone box to call the office to obtain where the next pick up was.

Monday was a quiet day and we could get some rest. To emphasise how busy we were, the Cortina Estate, which was brand new when we bought it, before it was a year old it had done 96,000 miles − that is more than most cars do in ten years.

To ease the burden and to develop the business we bought another new white Cortina, this time it was the saloon version. At a time when the average wage was about eight pounds per week, we advertised and offered drivers more than twice that amount. We soon had plenty of enquiries and we could pick and choose. A few months later we bought another white Cortina and then a fourth

Christmas was a very busy time. The first such holiday we operated White Cars by then we had two telephone lines, each phone was ringing constantly. As fast as we finished one call then the instrument would ring again. Jeans' mother, Ivy, had insisted on cooking us Christmas dinner, so we took the phones off the hook and spent half an hour eating it at the desk, but we did not have time to finish it. The operators at the exchange could send a loud whistle through the handset to show that it had not been replaced. It was not long into our break when this happened, restoring the receivers to their cradles and they immediately started to ring again.

After the holiday the G.P.O. which was part of the Post Office contacted us. (In the sixties it was the government body which supplied telephone lines.) We were told that we had brought Ilford's local telephone exchange to a standstill with over 5,000 people trying to get in touch with us. They advised White Cars to have more lines installed, which we did, ordering another four. By the end of that decade there were eighteen lines in use by the company.

To cope with the work, when a driver went out to pick up a fare and deliver them to their destination, the drivers, like myself, would find a phone box and call the office for another fare. There were no mobile phones then; it would be thirty odd years before they became the norm. In the office, which was the previous toy shop, there was a large table with a map of the area so the controller could plot the destination of each car – when they called in, he would be able to direct them to the nearest pickup.

The very familiar red telephone boxes were being altered at that time in that the mechanism was being changed from the type that had been established before the war. The new style, unlike the previous ones, now accepted 6d pieces (six pence) and timed out after a few minutes depending on the distance being called by the user.

This new format was quite different from the old devices, and there were still many of the old ones about. To call, you had to put two one penny pieces into a slot to make a connection, and when the other person answered, you pressed button 'A' to complete the link. A person calling locally could talk for as long as they wished. If they did not answer, then you pressed button 'B' and got your money back. But if you were calling long distance, then the arrangement was to speak to the operator, who would call the number you required and then they would inform you of the cost and waited for the coins to go in the box before completing the connection.

Because of our success and those in London, other people were opening similar minicab companies in different areas. A trick to stop possible fares coming to us at a cost of only two pence, was to go into a phone box with 'A' and 'B' push buttons, call our number, push button 'A' leaving the phone off the hook. This would then show our telephone as constantly engaged, which meant a potential client could not get through and would therefore call another company. Normally with six incoming lines it was not a real problem, but sometimes especially at busy times all six would be jammed up.

There was a need to improve our communications because of the ever increasing number of cars our company was using. We got in touch with Pye Telecommunications, who for a fee installed an aerial on the roof at Ley Street with two way radio units in all of the twenty odd cars. This solved two problems: not only could we send cars to their next job without waiting for them to call in, also if our incoming lines were blocked we had the addresses of most phone boxes and we could ask the drivers to check them out and replace the receivers if someone had used it and left the line open.

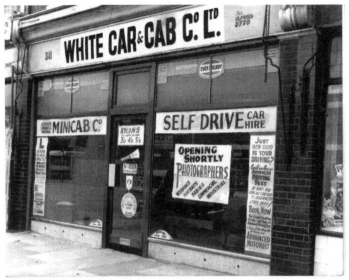

*Our Office which used to be our toy shop in
Ley Street, Ilford – it is also where we lived in the flat
above.*

Life was very good, we had a nice flat, lot of friends, a
young family and the business was flourishing and expanding.
Around about this time I took my Advance Driver's Test. After
two hours of driving around London with an examiner I
became a member of the Institute of Advanced Motorists. I
passed with one fault – I did not hold the steering wheel at the
ten to two position. I still do not hold it as recommended as I
find, and I guess most people do, tiring on long journeys. I
prefer to hold the wheel at the bottom with my arms in my lap,
restful and easy to respond to trouble. Incidentally, when
flying a light aircraft that is the position of holding the stick to
control it. And, of course, it should be remembered the ten to
two method of holding the steering wheel of a car came about
when vehicles were not so advanced as today. One needed to
hold the wheel firmly as it would twitch in your hand. Modern
day suspensions and tyres do not allow the road wheel to

follow a ridge in the road so most vehicles go straight without the struggle it used to be. And power steering makes it too easy.

**

One day we were approached by the pupils of the local Grammar school, they wanted our help as they had put a scheme together for Rag Week, and needed someone who looked a little bit more mature than they. Heinz Baked Beans had an advertisement on television in the sixties, where women lined up in the streets marching up and down singing ´Beans means Heinz´ and waving banners in the air with similar wording.

In Barking in East London and a few miles from the Grammar school there were about six high rise blocks of flats all of about twelve or fifteen storeys. Their idea was, to get all the housewives out of doors and march along the greens between the flats, whilst they pretended to film from the top of one of them; I was roped in with the film unit. It was hilarious – they organised the ladies to line up just like in the real advertisement, then the students had them marching up and down for about half an hour, singing ´Beans means Heinz´. The local college had designed the banners for the ladies to hold in the air just like the advert shown on TV.

They had informed the press beforehand who were taking pictures, which were published in the National newspapers. When Heinz, who had not been aware of the stunt, got to hear about it, no doubt through the media, they delivered cases of their products to the participants as compensation and a reward for the advertising.

**

In the mid to late sixties legislation was brought in by the Government to try and reduce alcohol related accidents on the

186

roads, and the dreaded breathalyser became the norm. In itself not an exact science as it is based on how much alcohol is in the body, not how the body handles it. It helped our business no end as the risk of being caught after a few drinks became very real. We started to get calls from Licensed Premises and also people would hire us just to go on a pub crawl. At that time businesses could put that down as a business expense for tax purposes on the basis they were entertaining clients. Unfortunately for us, this perk was removed a few years later and a lot of that work dried up.

We opened an office in Hackney in East London which gave us a problem with communication again as the transmission aerial on the roof of our office in Ilford was not high enough to cover that area. After waiting a few months the GPO installed a private telephone line from our Ilford base to Highgate Hill, the highest part of London. With the help of Pye we hired roof space on an office block on the brow of the hill to give us maximum radio coverage. I think it was an office block, but as I never went there it could, I suppose, have been a block of flats. When the work was finished, (by that time we had the use of over sixty cars) we were able to speak to them across the whole of the London Area, and in some instances a lot further than that. I can remember one driver calling in from as far as Brighton about sixty miles away.

Our customer base continued to grow and some big named firms were using our services. The jewel in the crown was when the Chief Executive, of the House of Commons Catering Department, started using White Cars on a regular basis, normally daily, to take him from his home in Essex to the Houses of Parliament in Westminster, and return when his days' work was finished.

As a result when the House was sitting late into the night, the many bars and restaurants in the premises would stay open for drinks or food for the M.P.s. Our friend from Essex, who was very secure in the service we offered, would order twelve or more cars with their drivers to wait outside the House of Parliament. When the Commons had finished its business, our drivers would take the staff home. I became not an infrequent visitor to his office near to the centre of the House becoming well known to the policemen, who stood at certain spots in the corridors. It made me feel good when I was saluted as I went past! I was also invited to their staff Christmas Parties.

On the other hand, as a result of our Hackney Office the infamous Kray twins who lived in that area, started to use our cars on a regular basis. They would sometimes order as many as five cars to take them around various clubs keeping our drivers and vehicles late into the night, whilst also paying them very well. Another regular user of our services was Sandy Shaw, who lived in Dagenham in those days; she was famous for performing in her bare feet and winning the European Song Contest singing `Puppet on a String´.

In Ilford High Road above Harrison and Gibson's Furniture Store was a restaurant called 'The Room at the Top' which dealt with fine food and had a resident band. Stan Slater was the general manager; he had a regular booking to take him home to South London, normally about one o'clock in the morning when the Room closed.

Stan and I got on well and he would invite me up to the restaurant to meet famous acts who performed for the guests in the ballroom. Names like Joe Brown and Dickie Valentine, popular singers of the time. The latter I had met in Kenya when he had toured the country to cheer up the troops. At first I found it embarrassing walking into the restaurant, the resident singer in the band would change the words to the song he was singing and sing 'here comes minicabs, here comes minicabs' before resuming to the proper words.

Stan and the head chef would after an invitation, attend parties we held at home, on special occasions they would supply the food. Once again I must say 'in the sixties' and as I mentioned earlier domestic fridges and freezers were not very common, in fact, virtually unheard of. One day Stan offered me an old Walls Ice Cream freezer which was surplus to their requirements. As I remember I paid the Room at the Top five pounds for it, which was equal to about half a week's average wage. We installed it in the garage and got some funny and questionable looks from friends, especially when we bought a whole cod and cut it up and stored it. Now any family would not be without one.

The sixties was a wonderful period full of excitement and new innovations. From the first man to go into space, Yuri Gagarin − a Russian in April 1961, the contraceptive pill was marketed in the same year. It was three years later when Mary Quant designed a skirt and named it after her Mini. In real terms it did not need much designing but exciting to see the ladies wearing them. The skirt was followed by hot pants, unusual to see in those days but every kid above ten seems to be wearing them at the time of writing. The Austin Mini motorcar became a cult vehicle, production started at the end of the fifties; it was very popular with celebrities and not unusual to see the little car with specialist paintwork, being driven around London and no doubt elsewhere. People were more relaxed and excited at all the new things which were happening; colour television, and even travelling abroad was becoming easier, and if you wanted to set up a business there was not a lot of red tape to prevent you.

By this time in the mid-sixties, we had formed the business into a limited company to protect us personally against unforeseen circumstances. We also changed the original name from White Car & Cab Company to White Cars (Essex) Ltd, and a similar company with London in the brackets. We did this because the licensed cab trade were not happy about the use of 'cab' in our name.

**

We had a few customers who were reluctant to pay, or to be kind, slow in paying. One, by the name of Stoller, was the managing director of a company which sold carpets; their head office and warehouse was near Liverpool Street Station close to the City of London. They also had a shop in Ilford High Road. I think they stopped trading years ago.

On one occasion, after some pressure from me, he stormed into our office one evening and showered the room with notes of various denominations by throwing them in the air. I took him to a local night club to calm him down, where he started to gamble. There was no limit on the tables and he started betting heavily, which made the management very happy and I was very popular. Suddenly their attitude changed as he was on a winning streak and was demanding to know if the house could cover what he was winning in cash. His winnings on roulette continued to climb and reached twenty-five thousand pounds and again he demanded to see the colour of their money as he wanted to bet the sum on double or nothing. After some chasing around, the house came up with the figure and he took the bet and lost. Losing twenty-five thousand pounds did not seem to bother him, in today's money I would guess it would be equal to half a million pounds.

He continued to use our services but again the account started to escalate. One day out of frustration as he was not responding to us, Jean and I went to his local shop and ordered the best Axminster Carpet they had in stock which was delivered the same day. The driver had wanted paying but I said no. Instead I called Stoller at their Head Office to ask for payment but he would not speak to me. I put the phone down saying "Tell him when he brings his account up to date, then you can have your carpet back", which was about twice the value of what was owed. He stopped using us and never returned our call, a year later we laid the carpet in our lounge. My one regret was it was a few inches too short to fit exactly.

The Club Cubana where I had taken Stoller was owned by two outfits, one side gambling was quite separate from the other which was owned by John Wilson. John was a lovely guy, very talented on the piano and full of fun, but his bills would sometimes get out of hand.

One very late evening knowing that John was on the way back from the West End of London in one of our cars, I parked around the corner and waited in his front garden for him to arrive. As he walked in the gate he was humming to himself and I could tell he had had quite a few to drink – he got a shock when he saw me standing there. He invited me in the house so we could discuss payment, but he did not have the 'ready cash' and the drinking club was run virtually on a hand to mouth basis. Sitting at his kitchen table with his wife asleep upstairs we discussed the problem over a bottle of Scotch. We finally solved how the club was going to settle its account with us – when I suggested we invited our regular customers to a party which the club would pay for, John agreed to the idea and we set a date for an evening when he would close the club except for people who had invitations issued by us.

Very shortly after we sent out invitations to our clients and prepared for the occasion hiring dinner suits for our management team. As our clients arrived, Jean and I was at the door to greet them, both of us dressed in evening wear, and a waitress offering them a glass of Champagne with a nip of brandy in it. John was brilliant on the piano and there was also a regular Jazz band. It was a great evening and helped to buy our customers loyalty, and for John he got new faces into his premises. It was so successful we repeated it the following year.

John was a special character and loved playing jokes. He had a set of revolvers, silver with white handles and he would walk around with them strapped to his waist, cowboy fashion. One time whilst in the club and for the hell of it, he did a quick draw of one of the guns and shot a hole in the floor, not realising it was still loaded.

It was one Christmas Eve when Jean, who was on control, received a phone call from the local police station to say John had been arrested for shooting someone. I was out on the road with a fare. The police said they would let him out on bail for five thousand pounds and he told them that I would be prepared put the money up and could I please go to the station to arrange it.

Jean spoke to me over the radio and my first thoughts were – where are we going to get five grand from? In today's money that is around, at a guess a hundred thousand pounds. Jean was asking me not to go, and if I did, not to commit us to bailing him out. As I went in the front entrance of the station, my thoughts were, if he is in trouble we will try and help him out, but I was not prepared to use finance to do it. The desk sergeant escorted me up some stairs which lead to the CID office, where he knocked on the door and somebody shouted "Come in." I was standing there thinking to myself *what was I going to say to him?*

The door was flung open and a big cheer went up, somebody put a glass of scotch in my hand and I joined the police stations annual party held in the detective room with bunting and Christmas decorations. John was there and thought it very funny, there were also other business people whom I recognised – I did not get a lot of work done that day, and Jean was most relieved when I phoned her and told her what it was all about.

The following year the annual party was held in a hall close to the rugby ground and I volunteered, for no fee, our mini coach to take people to it and home after.

**

In March of 1967 we were blessed with the arrival of Susan, but she much prefers to being called Sue, we now had two beautiful daughters, the love of our lives.

In the summer of that year I started training for a Private Pilots Licence, flying Rallye Clubs out of Biggin Hill in Kent. Biggin Hill was a very famous airfield during the war where Spitfires flew during and after the Battle of Britain. On the next page, is a page from my Pilots Log, the interesting entry is fifth up from the bottom. Part of the training is to learn how to get an aircraft out of a spin, which is when the plane stops flying and is just slipping through the air similar to a car sliding on ice and out of control. The Rallye Club which I was training in was a very gentle aircraft and not recommended for this form of flying.

| Date | AIRCRAFT | | CAPTAIN | Holder's Operating Capacity | JOURNEY or Nature of Flight | | Departure (G.M.T.) | Arrival (G.M.T.) |
|---|---|---|---|---|---|---|---|---|
| | Type | Registration | | | From | To | | |
| 25.10.67 | RALLYE CLUB | G. AVIM | J MARSHAL | P1 U/S | BIGGIN HILL | BLACKBUSH | 1630 | 1715 |
| — | " | G. AVIM | " | P1 U/S | BLACKBUSH | BIGGIN HILL | 1730 | 1800 |
| 22.11.67 | — | G. AVIM | — | P1 U/S | BIGGIN HILL | GATWICK | 1335 | 1400 |
| — | — | G. AVIM | — | P1 U/S | GATWICK | BIGGIN HILL | 1420 | 1510 |
| — | — | G. AVIO | — | P1 U/S | BIGGIN HILL R20 | BIGGIN HILL R20 | 1570 | 1570 |
| 6.12.67 | RALLYE continued | G. AVYS | P.U/S | BIGGIN HILL | — | LOCAL | 1525 | 1550 |
| — | — | — | — | P. U/S | — | — | 1505 | 1605 |
| 1.2.68 | TIGER MOTH | G-AOBO | P.J.HILL | P. U/T | BIGGIN HILL | BIGGIN HILL | 14.15 | 14.45 |
| 1.2.68 | RALLYE CLUB | G-AVVK | M DYNA | P. U/T | — | — | 1250 | 1335 |
| 16.2.68 | — | G-AVVK | C DYNR | P U/T | — | — | 1500 | 1550 |
| — | — | G-AVVK | C DYNR | P.U/T | — | — | 1600 | 1630 |
| — | — | — | J CHATTLEY | P 1 | — | — | 1630 | 1605 |

Grand Total, excluding Passenger Flying ......14...... hours .......55...... minutes.

The small occasional four seat mono-plane built in Toulouse by the same French firm that constructed part of Concorde. It's stall speed was very low for a fixed wing

194

aircraft around forty-five knots, in fact Brian Trubshaw, who was the chief test pilot for the supersonic airliner, demonstrated this during a very windy day at Biggin Hill, by flying into the wind, reducing power and the little plane was hovering above the runway.

To have practiced putting an aircraft into a spin with the Club the stresses would probably have torn its wings off so training was done in a twin wing Tiger Moth, first built before the Second World War. It was a beautiful bright day on the first of February; in the aircraft the seats are in tandem, also there is no canopy. On the ground it had been quite warm but at a few thousand feet with the wind singing through my hair it was bitterly cold, especially as I only had a suit on. I sat in the rear seat, with the pilot in the front cockpit who took the aircraft up to about three thousand feet. There was no radio in this ancient craft, communication between the front and back was through a talking tube, similar to what they used in the TV programme *Upstairs and Downstairs*.

After the climb he levelled the plane out and told me what was going to happen through the tube. He closed the revs of the engine to tick over and put the nose down. The plane almost immediately started to turn and was no longer flying, and we were going down vertically. The sensation is not one of the aircraft gyrating but that someone has taken hold of the corner of the ground, and spun it so that it was reeling in front of me like a spinning wheel.

The lesson is to train you how to get the aircraft flying again instead of slipping through the air. The first action is to stop the aircraft from going round and round so that it starts to respond to the controls. To do that, one uses the rudder in the opposite direction of the spin − once you have straightened the flight out, you pull the nose up gently before you hit the ground, which is coming towards you at about sixty miles per hour! The pilot demonstrated the method first and then I had to do the exercise three times before he passed me as proficient at it. Believe you me – you need a very strong stomach!

My greatest thrill though was the day which had started with just another lesson, this time doing circuits with the instructor sitting in the co-pilot's seat with me flying the aircraft. The lesson is to take off, go round the airfield, and land, but before stopping put the power back on and take off again.

After about the fifth landing he told me to stop the plane, I thought I had done something wrong and he wanted to lecture me about it. Instead as the plane came to a halt he opened the door and got out, saying something like, "Off you go I'll see you back in the office." It is recorded as the last entry on that particular page of my flying log.

Horror! The day I had been waiting for had arrived. All the knowledge and training vanished in an instant. There I was sitting in this multi-thousand pound aircraft and I was supposed to make it fly. But once in the air all the bad thoughts went and the excitement of being airborne and in control was very exhilarating. After which on other days the sheer thrill of flying solo round London is something not to forget or landing at Gatwick Airport amongst the big boys. On other occasions – just for the fun of it and, of course, keeping up flying hours flying off to Le Touquet in France for lunch.

I joined a Masonic Lodge somewhere around this time which brought many new friends one of which was George Sheppard, who owned a retired peoples home, and in the time I knew him he bought a thirty-four foot sea going sailing yacht from the Boat Exhibition in London.

I also met Jack Griffiths who had a science workshop in Ilford Lane; it is where he developed Sonic Testing which is a method whereby organisations such as the Ford Motor Company, who have a giant foundry, producing crank shafts for car engines from molten steel. Before Jack's invention, the company had to pull one in every hundred of the cranks apart by hydraulic means to see if there were any faults in the manufacturing process. With sonic testing each one of the units could be tested by sending an electrical note through it to see if there were any faults, if there was the note changed from a whistle to a dull sound. Similar to when checking to see if a glass container has a fault an expert flicks it with a finger, if it sings no problem, if it plonks it has a fault.

Jack had agents throughout the world and on one occasion he met directors from a Japanese Motor Manufacturer. The meeting was in a Chinese Restaurant just off Piccadilly Circus in London, which he invited me along to. He was concluding a deal for them to use his system, a very interesting afternoon. It was also the first time I had been in an Asian establishment where the food is laid out on the food warmers and one selects a small portion at a time from the turntable (a lazy Susan) in the middle of the dining table. Prior to that, the only Chinese restaurant I had been to was in East Ham High Street where the chicken chow mien came piled up on your plate.

Quite a few years later we were on our way to Lodge in the Connaught Rooms in London near to Charing Cross Station. We needed to pass the Old Bailey the famous central criminal courts which are not too far from St Paul's Cathedral. The IRA had exploded a car bomb outside the building doing extensive damage to it just prior to us passing. It was a time when the terrorists were very active and on that night they had also left a car bomb outside Scotland Yard, the Metropolitan Police Headquarters in London, along with a few others at important buildings, not all of which exploded. A small reminder of the war and the damage a bomb can create.

It was by rare chance, one morning I was in the front office in Ilford, doing some paperwork when three elderly ladies entered and to my surprise asked if we could take them to Italy. At first I thought they were having a laugh as we often got silly requests, normally from drunks, but not this early in the morning. It was when they explained that their brother used to drive them but he could no longer do so as he was in his seventies and his eyesight was not too good.

It turned out one of the three sisters was frightened of flying, so they needed to go by road. Also another was diabetic and had a need to eat frequently and there was no guarantee that could be achieved by any other form of transport. We had a discussion concerning cost and details of where they wanted to go in Italy which turned out to be in the North of the country at Lake Maggiore to a small village called Cannero Rivera.

At the time I did not realise that this would be the start of many more trips over the coming years to the charming lake surrounded by mountains, a beautiful climate with quaint little bars and restaurants and the clear waters with the odd ski boat skimming along.

So it was arranged, and early one morning I collected the ladies from their home in Ilford in my current car – a white Vauxhall Cresta which was a large comfortable car with six seats an automatic gearbox and power steering, both unusual extras for a car in the sixties. The picture above is the Viscount version, same shape but with more toys, leather trim and two-tone paint work, which ultimately I had two of.

The ride to Italy took two days. We had driven around London and on down to Ramsgate in Kent where we caught the fastest way to France at that time, the Hovercraft which could carry about fifty cars and took us to Calais in about thirty minutes, an hour quicker than the ferry. From there we drove through main roads as there were very few dual carriageways and also there were not many Auto routes.

We stayed the night in France at a quaint little hotel and then the following morning we made our way to the border with Switzerland, from which the last part of the journey was over the Simplon Pass into Italy – a total of just over 700 miles in two days. The three ladies were very pleased and recommended White Cars to friends and I did the journey a few more times. We informed the local newspapers of the trip for publicity. As a result the story went national and even the Readers Digest got in touch wanting to run pictures of the journey.

On returning to the UK the same evening, I had got off the Hovercraft in Ramsgate I was making my way to Epping along the road of the same name. There was a GT Cortina in front of me, otherwise the road was empty and I went to pass it. As I drew level with it, the driver accelerated. In front there was a bend in the road so I slowed up to drop behind him. But he did the same, so again I tried to pass him as I was in the middle of the road with this bend coming up rapidly. But again he did the same. I could see the lights of a car which was coming the other way, before we could actually see it. It came round the bend in the middle of the three lane highway. I was convinced it would move over into the empty lane, but it didn't, it just kept coming in the same part of the road I was on. It got closer and closer and we were due to hit head on. The Cortina was still on my left side so I could not move over.

One thing is certain − it is not good news to have an accident hitting someone head on but unfortunately I left it a few feet too late. She, it turned out to be a woman, stayed in the same lane, so I swerved to miss her trying to go up the empty road on her nearside. My nearside headlamp hit her nearside headlamp which brought the little Mini she was driving, to a stop, and spun it round in the road. I also spun off leaving the road and hitting a tree, the front end going into a deep ditch. The tree had buried itself in the driver's door which meant sliding across to get out of the passenger side. My only damage was a cut knee where an item on the key ring, hanging from the ignition had dug into it. The Cresta was no more. So I upgraded to the Viscount.

Prior to the above we had bought a motor cruiser, which was moored at a marina in the Crouch, a waterway in Essex which during the war had operated as an Air Sea Rescue Station, where fast motor launches were tied to a pontoon on the ready so they could race out to sea to pick up pilots who had been shot down over the waters. Our motor cruiser was twenty-four foot long, the problem being moored in the same spot on a river is that there is not anything new to see, and once you have cruised up and down a few times it gets a little boring.

Bradwell-on-Sea in Essex is situated on the mouth of the Blackwater, with lots more waterways to explore. A new marina had been built there and along with George's thirty-four foot sailing yacht, which also had been moored in the Crouch, we were the second and third boats to hire space at Bradwell Marina behind Englebert Humperdink's (a famous singer) vessel which was the first to be tied alongside the floating pontoons.

It was one of those dull summer days when we moved our cruiser, George had moved his boat the week before. Jean and Noreen, George's wife, drove us down to the Crouch, and were due to collect us from Bradwell the same evening. We had blankets and food with us just in case we got delayed and had to spend the night on board, as it was about a twelve-hour journey going down the river from the mooring and then out to sea, to miss the sand banks which are off the Essex East coast. Finally a left-hand turn (Port side) into the Blackwater and then up past the Nuclear Power station, and into the marina. To help with the gear we took our handyman, Joe, whose normal job was to repair any problems in our offices.

It was very dark when we arrived at Bradwell and we navigated into the new marina docking alongside the pontoon, which ran parallel with the shore. To get off the floating dock one needed to walk along it to a bridge that led up to the car park.

It was very dark as we disembarked leaving Joe to bring the bedding and to lock the boat. I turned just in time to see him walk towards the one light that was shining in the car park on the shore. He did not realise that there was a strip of water between the mooring and the land. He took a couple of steps, and before I could stop him he disappeared off the pontoon into the water.

What followed would have made a good comedy sketch for *Only Fools & Horses*. In rescuing him I went into the water, the bedding floated away and I ruined a soft leather jacket that I had just recently bought, the leather was fine but the lining disintegrated with the salt.

On leaving the yet unmade car park a large stone spun off a front wheel of the car, we heard the bang and did not think a great deal about it. It was not until we were on the way home when the automatic gearbox started slipping that is when I realised there was something wrong. The stone had hit the drain plug on the gearbox of the Vauxhall Viscount, allowing it to leak oil. It had been a great day which ended badly.

**

In 1970 and 1971 we took the family including my mother on holiday to Cannero on the side of Lake Maggiore, renting a ground floor flat which was owned by the ladies. On the first occasion we drove down as far as Rome, visiting the Vatican and staying at camp sites on the way. It was on this trip the Viscount broke down. A wheel bearing became noisy and was losing oil out of the axle. While we waited for the part to be flown out from the UK, we camped on a site near the town of Pisa and in the meantime we hired a local car. The part arrived a few days later but the people who had sent it had confused the order with a Vauxhall Victor part so when it arrived it did not fit.

We spent almost another week at the camp site, waiting for another bearing to be flown out from England. During that period we went to the famous tower; there were not too many tourists, and no charge to climb the circular staircase to the top. On a recent trip in 2011, the fee to go into the monument was 15 Euros per person, a big difference to the seventies. In the picture on the following page we are near the top of the Leaning Tower, with Jean, Sue and Anne − who is looking tired − it must have been the heat.

Before leaving England we had packed the car with tinned food to last the period of the holiday. I had discovered all sorts of places in the car to store the tins one of which was over the rear wheel arches and also lining the rear floor with them, with Mum and the girls in the back using them as foot rests. But by time we got to Pisa we were a little tired of eating every meal out of a variety of food packed in these containers. While out shopping we passed an Italian delicatessen and in the window were cooked chickens. We could not resist them and took of them back to the camp where we made a salad. But the chickens were uneatable to us because of the herbs and garlic they had been cooked in. Today the taste we would enjoy and would not be a problem. We had two of the birds and we gave them both away to the local Italian people. They were very pleased.

While our car was being repaired we hired a Fiat. One day I was on my own when I drove into the local town, I'm not certain what I had done wrong although I think it was crossing a single white line. Two Motorcycle Policemen roared past me and then swerved in front and told me to stop. Because of the Italian plates on the car and in a period when there were very few English tourists, there was a shocked look on their faces when I showed them my blue (as they were in those days) very English passport and they realised I did not understand what they were talking about. Eventually one of them took a Lira note out of his pocket to show me what he wanted. I took it and said 'thank you' or something like that and put the note in my pocket. All hell broke loose! The next minute the handcuffs came out, so I thought I should give in and pay them the traffic fine they were asking for.

Eventually the part arrived from England and with reluctance we packed all our gear into the car and made our way to our ultimate destination of the Lakes in the north. One very important thing we did learn on that holiday was do not wear yellow because it attracts the wasp to you.

During that trip and before the car broke down, we had stopped at a camp site near to the Italian Border with France. It was extremely hot and the walkways of the sands had boarding over them so your feet would not burn. We set up our regular two tents on what was a dusty dry day. The site was not really to our liking, there was a funny feeling about the place. Nevertheless, we had travelled a long way so we got our pitch ready, Mum in one tent with the two girls, Jean and I in the other.

There was a very big swimming pool which had a large stone statue to one side, to which I took the girls, so they could cool off. I sat on the side whilst they played in the water which was of equal depth across the pool. I was on my own sitting on some steps and I think I was dozing in the heat. Anne woke me with a start by tugging my arm. She didn't say anything but just pointed to the pool where Sue, about three years old at the time, was floating face down.

The water came up to my knees, and was slapping around my legs as I rushed through the throng of children who were playing in the sun. Picking Sue up I discovered she wasn't breathing. I carried her quickly to the side where I laid her face down and started to rub her back − suddenly she was very sick bringing up lots of water. She was fine after that, but as tired as we were we packed everything in the car and moved on. Anne explained afterwards that someone had pushed her and she had hit her head on the smooth stone statue and fell into the water. The result was that she had a large bruise on her forehead for a few days.

Italy taxed fuel very highly and was the most expensive in Europe. In order to encourage tourism, the Italian Government issued vouchers through their embassies, which could also be bought at AA offices. In other words, you prepaid for your fuel before going on holiday but it was free of their very high tax rate. On the rear of these vouchers was the terms and conditions in various languages, including English and Italian. These terms and conditions clearly stated that in no circumstances should you pay any more for your fuel than the value of the voucher.

We were staying in Cannero Rivera and thought we would visit the other lakes around that area, the one that was most known was Como, so we made our way there. In the morning we left it had been on the news that Italy had increased its taxes including motor fuel. I did not take too much notice – as we had our vouchers.

In that part of the world there is some beautiful scenery which we were admiring as we made our way through the countryside. The fuel gauge was getting low, no rush but I was on the lookout for somewhere to fill up. At the bottom of a hill on a bend there was a petrol station with just one pump. Over to the left of a wide area there was a café, outside of which was a motorcycle belonging to the Carabinieri, the Italian police, which did not bother us in the least.

I pulled up alongside the petrol pump and handed over the vouchers to show the young lad how much fuel I needed. When he finished he asked for more money than the value on the voucher. I said no and pointed to the rear of the ticket showing him in his language and mine what the wording said 'On no account pay any more money than the value of this ticket.' Or words to that effect certainly in the English translation, I assumed the Italian version was the same. He got very annoyed and called over his boss, an elderly man. Again I was not concerned as I had great faith in the system and the wording. After a very brief exchange with the newcomer showing the wording on the back, he said something to the boy and he ran off to the cafe. The Policeman (*Carabinieri*) came out of the snack bar, and then a police car arrived and I was arrested for trying to defraud the petrol station owner. One of the officers drove my car with the family in it and they put the car with the contents into a locked yard. Where they all came from I do not know.

Now, in England that would not happen as the police would say it is a civil matter and nothing to do with them. I was taken to the police station and put in a cell, with grey steel walls which was all very frightening. After some time they found someone who spoke very good English and Italian, but that did not get me any further. In the end I paid the difference and they let us go. But in some ways I got my own back, as I still had a lot of these vouchers and I sold them to some friends of the ladies.

# The Association

By the mid-sixties there were similar companies to ours throughout London with the same strict rules concerning car worthiness, driver ability and insurance cover. One day I had a telephone call inviting me to go to a meeting in South London to form an association to try and clean up the industry. The National Radio Car & Private Hire Association was formed, I never did like the name − it was too long and clumsy.

The Association started to take up more and more of my time. One of the biggest problems all companies had was motor insurance especially for owner drivers. Most days I was involved on Association work as I had been voted to be its President. The organisation itself was very new and I was still finding my way about and trying to make decisions of what was needed to be done.

There were no easy payment terms for insurance cover, the annual fee had to be paid up front and it was very expensive which precluded many people who wanted to take up driving with their own vehicle. We needed to find an answer to this problem.

Other problems were escalating. The industry was getting a bad name, in that small firms that had opened up were not fussy about what sort of vehicles they used, and did not worry themselves about insurance or their cars being roadworthy − and some firms were even using seriously worn out cars. We set up a system so members could be recognised by displaying a badge on the windscreens. But the organisation was not strong enough, and with the committee members all busy with their own companies, it was only me that was doing any work which was detrimental to our own business.

**

The flat in Ley Street, although large and nicely furnished, was claustrophobic in the sense there was nowhere for the girls to play, especially as it was on a main road, also there was no back garden to speak of. To get out in the air and let Anne and Sue run around we used to find time on a Sunday to go over to Valentines Park, a large open space with a boating lake not too far from our home.

We started to look for a house to buy, but it turned out not to be so easy as there were more buyers than houses for sale, and although we had agreed to buy on a number of occasions, somebody else would make a better offer, and the deal would fall through.

Because I was very busy Jean was driving around looking at different properties, one day she phoned me saying that she was at this house in View Close, Chigwell and if we could give the seller a deposit it would be ours. The house was all we were looking for: it was detached on a corner plot with a large garden and not very old, with four bedrooms, a large kitchen and a separate dining room, everything that we wanted. We eventually moved in.

**

We had bought a Rolls Royce, a beautiful car with a cocktail cabinet in the rear which was ideal for weddings. On one occasion I picked the bride and groom up from the famous wedding facility at Caxton Hall in the centre of London and took them out to Hertfordshire for the wedding reception. We arrived at this large house, and as I had to wait to take some people back to Ilford, I was invited in.

On a long reception table there were about a dozen or so bottles of Champagne, which someone had removed the wires from the corks before the guests had arrived. It was a warm day with the sun shining through the window and on to the table, it looked grand with the bottles glistening in the light. However, the pressure in the bottles was rising....

The bride, in her wedding outfit came into the room arm in arm with her new husband, and they were standing near the table admiring the cake and layout. There was a loud 'POP', and then another as all the bottles blew their corks out with champers jetting into the air and going everywhere; I was still laughing when I got home. I think somebody learned a lesson that day as to why champagne bottles have wires on them.

We had been receiving enquiries for a vehicle to move caravans, and when I was offered a Land Rover for a reasonable price I bought it. I don't remember it doing a lot of work, but my brother Bob, whose wife lived near Bude in North Devon took it home with him one weekend. Evidently he thought it would be a bit of fun to drive it across the vast sands in that area. Somehow he managed to bog the vehicle down and with all four wheels spinning he could not extract it and the tide was on the turn. The water swallowed the Land Rover up and it disappeared below the surface, so much so the Coast Guard put a buoy over it to warn shipping − alright the fishing boats which would be making their way into Barnstable. He told me he got in touch with the local Army which was a REME unit and they used it as an exercise to recover it after the water had receded. After my experiences with the Land Rover in Kenya, my thoughts were, 'that I did not understand how he got it bogged down.'

\*\*

The Italian ladies introduced us to a couple who wanted to move to Italy. Using one of our Transit vans I agreed to move their belongings.

At that time there was a coach service that went from London to Paris, perhaps it still does? I suggested to Jean that if she waited a few days to allow me to deliver our clients to their new home, I would drive back through France and meet her in Paris so we could spend a few days in the French City.

The journey in the van did not go too well, and I broke down on the Simplon Pass which goes across the Alps from Switzerland into Italy. The Pass at the time was very narrow with passing places for vehicles coming in the opposite direction. The engine on the van had started to overheat and when it started to boil I closed it down.

At that point we were about fifteen miles from the top, which by now was unreachable so the only way was down, as we had no communication to call for help. It had got dark and we could not stay where we were at snow level, it was bitterly cold and without the heater blowing warm air from the engine, we would have frozen. I rolled the van down backwards, for there was nowhere to turn it on the steep narrow pass. To achieve it I leant out of the driver's door looking backwards, controlling the decent using the brakes and steering. I got a stiff back which lasted a few days − my passengers were terrified. Trying to see where I was going was not too difficult as the road bends and twist, giving me a clear view if something was coming up behind us. Eventually a car did come along and the driver helped me to turn the van around, in one of the passing places, so we arrived at the bottom going forward but still freewheeling. When we entered the town at the base of the hill, to my relief, I saw the local Ford dealer and he was open. The van needed a head gasket replacing. It was taken into their workshop where they repaired it overnight. What a brilliant service.

I was very well delayed and there was no way to get in touch with Jean. To telephone England at that time from the Continent, one had to wait for various operators to put you through and it could take most of the day. Finally, I managed to deliver the clients to their new home and now I could make my way to Paris.

The journey from Italy to Paris was difficult; the Transit had a flat-sided Luton over the driver's cab which slowed the journey as there was a strong head wind. It took a lot longer than expected, especially as I had more trouble with the vehicle when I got out of the cab without cancelling the alarm and it would not let me back in. The only way was to smash a quarter light in the door window, put my hand in to the switch under the dashboard and turn the alarm off − so I could open the door.

Jean was staying at the hotel next to the main railway station in the city. A friend who lived in Paris had booked the room and I knew the number that she was staying in. When I finally got there forty odd hours late and very tired, there was a queue at the desk; knowing the room number and I could see the key hanging on the hook behind the receptionist, so I walked to the front of the queue and took the key and went to her room.

You can imagine my surprise when I got there and a male jacket was hanging over a chair and girly magazines on the bed. It turned out Jean had not liked the room and had been moved to a nicer one.

**

George's boat was sea going, a Dufour 35, with all the equipment to sail safely, he eventually retired and sailed it to Ibiza, but a long time after this story. Ours, although it had six berths and was quite happy at sea, the six cylinder diesel was a bit expensive to run, long journeys were not practical.

On an occasion in November having a glass or two in a bar, George and I decided to sail to Oostende in Belgium, to get some sailing practice in. We studied the charts and the tides and we came to the conclusion it would be better to leave in the evening catching the falling water to help us on the way.

We took the craft out of the difficult entrance to the marina checking everything was in order. We knew what the compass bearings were. As it would be an overnight crossing we would take it in turns to navigate while the other rested. While George got his head down, so he could take the next watch, he issued me with navigation instructions and we were off, and I was to wake him at a certain point.

I do not know how boats find their way around today, probably by GPS, but then it was by compass and Admiralty sea charts.

I took the boat down the Blackwater and out to sea. George's instructions were to sail at a certain compass bearing and after about half an hour I would see a buoy with a flashing light and to aim for it. Each one flashes in a ten second sequence a serious of coded lights so it is possible at night to read this sequence to confirm your whereabouts.

Sure enough there it was. The night was pitch black, which made it difficult to judge distances. The waves in the water were not too rough and I sat in the cockpit with the tiller in my hand, keeping an eye on the compass and watching the light which was steadily coming towards us – I was mesmerised with its constant flashing. Suddenly, it was just in front of the yacht; its bright white light reflecting off the sails.

It was large, taller than the boat, the light flashing on and off in a certain coded pattern, to show its name as marked on the charts. We were sailing slightly into the wind, I quickly swung the rudder over hoping we would go round it, but I had turned the wrong way and it did not happen. We hit it just behind our starboard bow and the thing slid down the side of the boat in a bouncing movement with loud 'BANG, BANG, BANG' before it was behind us.

George came rushing up from below and shouted, "I told you to aim for it not f******g hit it!"

The buoy had a very thick rubber type band around it which prevented any damage, we sailed on. It was a very frightening experience for both of us, sinking in the North Sea in November would not have been funny. Unfortunately the wind dropped and in the middle of the month and mid-winter we became becalmed over the other side of the English Channel with not even a breeze to help us along, we had to return using the inboard diesel engine. There was not enough fuel to take us all the way back to Bradwell, but by taking the shorter crossing to Ramsgate was manageable.

From the boat I made a telephone call via the coastguard to my office and arranged for a car to pick us up leaving the boat moored in the dockside. I thought it funny as there was no Customs or other officials to welcome us asking for details of where and what we had been doing. The few days were an adventure and fun but turned out to be very disappointing as we did not achieve much sailing practice.

\*\*

The Association made a deal with an insurance broker in West London who agreed to arrange cover for our members on a monthly basis, and at the same time provide office space for the organisation. This to my mind was a step in the right direction, and we took up the offer.

It turned out the space was far too small it was more like a cupboard than an office. Another problem: it was also taking up too much time travelling into London to carry out any work on Association business, which sometimes only needed an hour or a little longer. To save the travelling and the time in going into London for a few hours' work I was doing it at my own desk.

So although we had partly solved the insurance situation it was not very satisfactory. The Association had another problem with funding – nobody or any company was prepared to pay for its running expenses.

We at White Cars were in the throes of reorganising by closing the Hackney office and running the company from Ilford, which was possible because we still kept the communication facility on Highgate Hill. At a committee meeting of the Association I made an offer that if they allowed me to sell motor insurance to the members, I would donate the Hackney office for the running of the Association and pay a commission from each sale for day-to-day running costs.

My offer was accepted with the one proviso that Ron Williams should be involved as the Associations Secretary. As I had already discussed my plans with him and agreed in principle this was not a problem. Our office in Hackney changed from a cab office to an insurance agency and the Association's Head Office.

In Ilford with the telephone facilities transferred from Hackney, there were eighteen incoming lines. To cope with the calls that they generated we had installed three pairs of desks for telephonists, with a six inch wide conveyer belt running between them. When a booking was accepted a slip was written out with the details and put on the belt which took the address to the controller, who would direct a car or cars to the pick-up.

**

The Association had approached Heathrow Airport for facilities so that our members could pick up passengers. As I stated earlier, the difference between minicabs and other cabs that roamed the streets, was that we had to be pre-booked or a prospective fare could instantly hire a car from an office or parking area. In theory the licensed trade operating out of the Airport were acting similar to the private hire trade in that they lined up in a rank waiting for a fare.

I, with Ron, acting as the Associations Secretary spent a lot of time talking to officials and the CEO at the Airport persuading them to allow a parking facility where people could hire a car, explaining that it was no different to what the taxi trade were doing. We had put a scheme together where an officer from the Association would be at the airport to monitor and control the use and ensure only member cars, that were properly regulated, would use the facility. At that time before the underground train service was extended to Heathrow, the authority there had a problem with moving people efficiently, and with our facility it would mean a few more folks could be transported. We were shown charts in their offices which were projecting passenger movements over the next ten years, and they were expanding rapidly doubling to around twenty-three million, and the infrastructure could not cope with the expansion. The airport agreed to our proposals, with the result of the ground floor of the car park at Terminal 'A' was fenced off with steel barriers for the use of our members.

It all fell apart before it got started when one of our member's cars used the licensed cab rank to pick up a fare. The airport, which had only been lukewarm about the idea, backed off after the row that erupted from the licensed cab drivers. Because of one person's action it spoiled what would have been a great scheme for everybody, and no doubt, a facility in every airport today offering a competitive service to that of taxis.

**

The insurance company, Union Accident, were not very happy with the London Brokers who were selling their facility.

They suspected that members were being sold cover which the insurance company were not being paid for, and I was invited to visit the insurers, without the brokers, to discuss the problem.

Today everything in the insurance world is done electronically but then it was all done by hand, and if a cover note was written out and the copy was not sent to the insurer, then a charge for the premium to the broker would be missed. The insurers had a check as cover notes which ran in numerical sequence, so in theory, it was not possible to cheat but there were too many loopholes.

Whilst it is very illegal to back date a cover note, it was too simple to write one out and declare to the insurer that it had been written out in error, or cancelled because of non-payment by the insured. But the insurance company was getting too many of these and were suspicious.

At long last things were moving in the right direction. I made a deal with the insurer that if they offered us a brokerage we would sell cover directly to our members. We were able to set up a unique deal, a first in the industry in which we were able to cover a vehicle for just three months, so instead of paying for an annual policy the fee was reduced in accordance with the risk. Initially, each policy lasted for three months, and then could continue to run monthly or at a discount annually. We became the N.R.C. Insurance Brokers.

It was in 1970 we started to publish a magazine for the trade and in the following pages is the initial copy and further ones in a different format and some articles published at that time; they are worth reading for what happened next.

On the following page is a copy of the Association's first newsletter it was later renamed POB a common phrase in the industry meaning 'Passenger on Board' which a driver would use over the radio when they had picked up their fare.

# NATIONAL RADIO CAR

**Published by The National Radio Car & Private Hire Association in the interest of the trade and its users.**

9th October 1970      Price: ONE SHILLING      Vol. I No. I

## EDITORIAL

There have been plenty of happenings recently that are worth mentioning, we moved into our first office at 25, South Molton Street, in the same building as the Association's Insurance Brokers, Hodges Fry Ltd. Already we are finding space short and are planning moving to larger premises, more about that at a later date.

During July, Ron Williams, the National Secretary, and myself had an appointment with Michael English, M.P. for Nottingham, at the House of Commons, who has been active in many ways with regards to legislation for the car hire trade. We had a very interesting meeting exchanging opinions and we will be seeing him again in the new session of Parliament.

I also had occasion to visit the House of Commons a second time in July this time with Roy Hatton, Eastern Area Secretary, to discuss the Bill which the Borough of Southend are putting through Parliament. This Bill has a section dealing with the car hire trade which we feel treats our members in Southend very unfairly. The meeting was with the two M.P.s for the Borough, Sir Stephen McAdden and Paul Channon, and we were able to put forward our point of view. They will be discussing these points with the Southend Borough Council and we hope to hear from them with their reply in the near future.

Now that we have got a news letter which will be circulated to member companies monthly, perhaps we can have some ideas from you the readers, stories — jokes — anything of interest to the trade, but please let us have them in writing, NO telephone calls.

At the moment I am dealing with a problem which St. Johns Car Service at E.17 have, regarding the Trades Descriptions Act. The Weights & Measures Inspector has warned them about distributing Association cards, the one that reads "National Radio Cars" across the top. The Inspector seems to think that this is misleading to the public as our member does not have radios in his cars. I have had a long telephone conversation with the Inspector but he wants to meet our member and ourselves before he makes a final decision. I will let you know the result in the next issue.

We have applied to the G.P.O. for a heading in the telephone directory under "National Radio Cars", each member will have a separate entry after the district he operates from, the districts will be in alphabetical order. There will be a circular explaining this more fully when we have all the details from the G.P.O.

Lastly, would all members who are in arrears with their subscriptions please pay immediately, we need the money and please note that the subscriptions from Associate Members is now £1.

P. CHATTEY, President

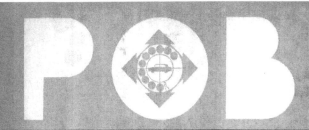

May 1971        Vol. 2 No. 1

# N.R.C.

## *Insurance Brokers*

### The Reliable
### Nationwide
### Insurance
### for
### Private Hire

 *Immediate Cover - 985 5341*

### Plus
### RADIO INSURANCE

P.O.B is published by the National Radio Car & Private Hire Association. Head Office. 347 Wick Road, London, E.9.
Telephone: 01 - 985 5341

# As I see it
## - by Percy Chattey -

Congratulations to "Steering Wheel", the journal of the British Taxi industry which celebrates its 50th anniversary this year. Many thanks too to Joe Toff the editor of "Steering Wheel" for his letter to us giving his best wishes.

Although it may seem that we are on the verge of running a mutual admiration society the taxis and the private hire boys are not quite, as yet anyway, as close and as friendly as may seem. But it is a beginning.

What we do appear to be building in each other's publication is a continual cross reference to articles that appeared in previous or concurrent issues. For instance I wrote an article on the Maxwell Stamp Report in the March issue. In the May 15 issue of "Steering Wheel", Arthur Goldwater goes all out to tear my piece apart. And here I am now having a go at them for a report on certain goings on at the Europa Hotel. As long as this type of reporting stays on a factual and adult level it's probably a good thing. It gives everybody a chance to air their views and somewhere along the line we might find ourselves agreeing which, as Oscar Wilde had one of his characters say, "Ah! don't say that you agree with me. When people agree with me I always feel that I must be wrong".

However, it would appear that a private hire firm managed to come to an arrangement with the porters at the Europa Hotel that they could telephone them when a guest wanted a car. I don't know if it was a member company or not. Naturally the cab-boys were rather put out as the private cars arrived to take people off sight-seeing or to the airport. Not that they had too much time to stay that way as the traffic from London Hotels is always so brisk that the demand exceeds the supply of transport.

As taxi-man Ted Solomons reports the incident in question a private hire vehicle arrived at the hotel and was loaded up with baggage. When the guest and his wife, a South African travel agent from Johannesburg, came out the conversation went like this, "Where's my luggage," Porter, "On the taxi, sir". "What's the bloody game? Don't you think I know what a London taxi looks like? Get my luggage out of there."

The offending luggage was removed and placed on Mr. Solomons's taxi. The South African guest (As we know South African guests are well known for speaking their unprejudiced minds) then gave his opinion of the situation, "There's some fiddle going on here." Mr. Solomons agreed with him.

The outcome of this is the suggestion that taxi-men boycott the Europa Hotel.

Here we have an instant storm in a plastic tea-cup. As we all know there is not a hotel in London that does not, from time to time, use private hire cars. In the same way as Public bodies, large companies and even Parliament do. Sometimes it is a matter of taste, some people prefer travelling in a saloon, other times it is expediency—there are no cabs around. The reverse can happen, a private vehicle is called and when it arrives the driver finds the passengers have taken cab instead.

The basis for this complaint seems to be the suggestion that a bribe was at the bottom of the hiring. In other words the porters pick up a commission for calling the private hire car. As a Mr. Sam Goldstein is quoted in the article, "Obviously the porters are on the make".

I think Mr. Goldstein is quite right. The porters are being paid a commission. Naughty.

To change the subject, I love the advertising in "Steering Wheel" and in their competitor "Taxi". On page 11 of "Steering Wheel" taximen are offered 75p COD for every accepted booking at the Hotel Beverley Towers. As the ad says, "It pays you to drive straight to . . . .". Another high moral standing ad says, "£3 extra for you". That is if they introduce clients to the Emerald Staff Consultants.

In "Taxi" an advertisement placed by the Tudor Room offers high commission and a £2 voucher towards a free holiday in the U.S.A.

Now I think that maybe the other hotels in London and the clubs and the employment bureaus are going to do some boycotting themselves. "There's a fiddle going on here." I can hear them say. "Taxidrivers are taking bribes."

Who is to say the hotel or club or whatever is any better than the established ones. Is it fair that when a driver has a passenger who asks his advice about where to go or stay that he is influenced purely by what commission he is going to get out of it?

How is it that a publication can run a story with quotes that call for drastic action because a porter picks up a commission and yet take money from advertisers who offer far higher rewards for taking passengers to what, to them, is an unknown destination? What was that about conflicting vested interests?

"Whats 28p divided by five?"

# A Deadly Fire

Hopefully, if you the reader has read this far, and has read the articles as published in the POB magazine above, then they will understand that there was no love lost between the private hire trade and the licensed taxi operators.

To continue the story we need to go back to when we were still living in the flat above the office in Ley Street. We had a direct internal telephone line down to the control room; it was not unusual to have a call in the night when the controller was short of cars.

On one particular night it was about two o'clock when I answered the phone to David Edwards who was on control duty. He was asking me for a quote to take someone to Nottingham, in my sleep I thought of Northampton. It turned out to be a lady that had fallen out with her partner, and was standing on a roundabout just off the Eastern Avenue, in Ilford with no bags or coat and wanted to be taken to her Grandmother's house.

That was a very expensive misquote as Nottingham is twice the distance. On top of which it was a terrible journey, they were building the M1 motorway at the time and it was road works all the way. When I picked her up I expected to be back early morning, but it was not until later in the day when I returned.

**

Despite the German bombers in the Second World War, which destroyed about a third of the housing stock in London, there were still a lot of Victorian terrace houses, some with shop fronts to the ground floor which represented the shopping areas of the past.

One of these was in High Street, Honiton, an area of London not very far from Hackney. The premises, like the district was very run-down and it had been a long time since anyone had traded from it. That was until someone, nothing to do with us, opened a minicab office on the third and top floor of the building. The small shop area on the ground floor, which one had to walk through to get to the stairs, was littered with rubbish from the last occupier.

Harry, a lovely, friendly, down to earth guy who had managed our Hackney branch knew the people who had opened this office and sometimes he would visit them. It was late one night, Jean and I had gone to bed leaving Fred Kauter, our Ilford Manager and one of our first employees, on control. The internal phone beside our bed started to ring, it was Fred telling me that there had been a serious fire in Hackney and people were injured.

At first I thought it was our place, and things like insurance cover, had we renewed it, started running through my head. It was a relief to be told that it was this other office, not knowing at that time the full horror of what had taken place that night.

We got out of bed and it was decided that Jean would take over the control while Fred and I would go and investigate to see what had happened. It took about twenty minutes to get to the site and by the time we got there the fire was almost under control with smoke still pouring from the upper floor windows, it was obvious the building was gutted.

As we arrived the last of the ambulances was taking away a body in a body bag. We learned later that Harry and two other drivers had gone there to celebrate someone's birthday. We stood there in shock looking at this extraordinary scene, trying to keep out of the way of the fire fighters, their hose pipes lying across the ground from the various red fire engines parked adjacent to the burning building.

The police revealed that the fire had been reported by a taxi driver who had been passing and had seen the fire flickering through the dirty stained glass of the old shop front window on the ground floor. The place was like a tinder box. With no doors to stop it the fire had swept up the wooden staircase gathering enormous intensity and speed.

There were eight occupants in the office and they had opened the windows calling for help. The fire swept through the room killing all the occupants. One person had tried to escape by jumping out of the window but was dead when he hit the pavement. We were told the fire would have consumed all the oxygen in the building and the occupants would have died from asphyxiation

The police, when they knew who we were, asked us if we would identify the bodies. We followed the police to the morgue where all eight had been laid out on separate beds in open body bags but they were too badly burned to be able to recognise any of them. It was a horrible sight and we left without being of any help in their work of recognition.

One of the drivers, who had gone to the party with Harry, lived in Collier Row, near Romford in Essex, who should have finished his shift at midnight. We were on the way back to the Ilford office, when Jean called over the radio and said the wife of this driver had called a few times to find out where he was.

We had been assured by the police that the next of kin would be informed very quickly, but an hour later, when we were back in the office and it was just getting daylight, when she phoned again. We telephoned the police in Romford asking them if they were arranging a visit to inform her of the tragedy, but they had no information and the Hackney Police had not been in touch.

There was no alternative but to go to her, for it would be wrong to tell her over the phone what had happened. Fred took over control again and Jean and I went to her home. We pulled up outside a lovely semi-detached house in a tree-lined street. The property was well kept and we walked up the path to the front door which was recessed under a tiled porch.

The door was opened very quickly, she stood there with a look of sheer terror on her face, she knew something bad had happened and started to scream. We contacted the next door neighbour who came in to help and after a while she took the two little children into her house. She had also phoned the doctor and we waited for him, he gave the wife a sedative to help her.

Other friends arrived to look after her and it was time for us to leave. It was about this time we learned that her parents were on holiday in a caravan and there was no way she could get in touch with them. We asked where the caravan park was, and we were told it was near Southend which was about thirty miles away, Jean and I drove there to give the parents the bad news.

All the newspapers carried the story the following day – most making it a war between the taxi and minicab owners, especially as it had been a taxi driver who had reported the fire in the first instance. The final verdict was that someone entering the building had discarded a lighted cigarette stub in the rubbish strewn across the ground floor... but we will never know.

The funeral took place at the City of London Cemetery in Manor Park, East London, the cortège was very long as there were many drivers wanting to show their respect and used their cars to do so, and one report said the line of cars stretched for two miles.

# Government Discussions

In 1972 the beloved British currency was changed from pounds, shillings and pence, to pounds and new pence, a simpler form of accounting making the introduction of Value Added Tax (VAT) that much easier. This was to replace the existing purchase tax as from 1974.

I was invited to the Government's Treasury Department to discuss how this new tax was to be applied to the car hire trade. Before that date, beside normal taxation and fuel tax, there was no tax for offering a service payable in the industry, and it was with a shock when I learned VAT was to be added to all services. Quite frankly I could not see how it would work. After three visits and discussions, where I was allowed to put the case for the private hire industry, while sitting around a large teak-coloured table talking to civil servants. The decision was made that for our type of trade, which is mainly cash, there was no sure way to make it work in practice, and the cost to monitor it was not practical. At one stage I thought they were going to apply it to account customers, but it did not happen.

I had also been to Whitehall (government offices) on other occasions, one of which was to be interviewed by the Maxwell Stamp Committee. This committee had been set up by the authorities to look into how the taxi trade and the car hire trade worked and should there be any changes. This committee had been instigated by the licensed taxi trade who were trying to ban the use of private vehicles being used to transport fare paying passengers. They had put up all sorts of reasons from worn out cars, uninsured ones and drivers without any training. In some ways I could see their point, because to become a licensed taxi driver in London took years of training.

Much to the taxi operators disgust the committee came out in our favour, although they did get their way when it was decided that the word ´cab´ could only apply to a vehicle that plied for hire on the streets, referring to how the use of the word first came in to use in the nineteenth centenary. This decision did not affect our company as we had already dropped the word from our advertising a few years before relying on our trade name of White Cars. Other companies changed their names from minicabs to minicars, not much difference in real terms.

I was also having meetings with Michael English, MP for Nottingham, at the House of Commons; he was acting for the Association and had put his name down for what is known as a 'Ten-Minute Bill'. The intention of this bill was to force car hire companies to use approved vehicles and to set up a licensing system for their use. It all came to pass a long time later. But by then, unfortunately, I was not involved and also Michael was no longer an MP.

In the early seventies as explained earlier, we moved to a four bedroom detached house in Chigwell, not too far from where Bobby Moore lived, who captained the English football team which won the World Cup in 1966. Our MP friend, Michael on a number of occasions came in the evening for dinner and normally our good friend Eddie, our solicitor, and Sonia his wife who lived not too far away in Epping, would join us.

**

In the wilds of Exmoor in Devon there is a small hamlet called Challacombe, it consists of a few cottages, a quaint little inn, a phone box and a shop.

John Green the landlord of the inn, we had known for some time as he was the tenant in a hostelry in Mortehoe near Woolacombe in North Devon. His pub at that time was not far from where our caravan was sited, where we had stayed for a break when we ran the toy and cycle shop.

The picture on the next page is the Ring O´ Bells and when it came on the market, John bought it, changed the name back to the original Black Venus, a reference to the ancient days when it was a hideout for smugglers. A problem he had in the bar was that you had to have your head bowed as the ceiling was very low, so he dug the dirt floor out and tiled it. As the ceiling was still not very high he hung thick leather straps from it, like the ones in a railway carriage. It was strangely very comfortable hanging on one with a drink in the other hand while chatting.

In 1969 we took three months off and stayed in Devon some of the time enjoying the delights of the tiny village. One time I tried to teach Jean how to fire a shot gun and handle the recoil. One shot and the backlash from the firearm sent her stumbling backwards, after which she went off the idea. In the afternoon when the pub was closed we would go with John and our two children, to the beaches at Combe Martin.

John, always the joker, whose idea of breakfast was honey and cider! One day whilst sitting in the sun in a small cove, the tide started to turn and I knew that the beach would be covered in water and would block any path off out of the area. John carried on dozing saying not to worry, when suddenly he jumped up, dived into the water and disappeared. We were stranded, the water had risen blocking the way out.

*Black Venus*

We stood looking around wondering what had happened to him. He had dived into the water and gone beneath the surface, and vanished, while the tide was still rising. The cliff behind us was tall and ragged with no paths. After about fifteen maybe twenty minutes of panic he came round the corner in a rowing boat. He had swum under the water around the corner of the cliff out of our sight, to get to the boat. He thought it was very funny; I was not so happy, especially when he pushed me in complete with sports jacket and trousers, as I was sitting on the edge of the vessel, much to the delight of the children.

Once a fortnight I would drive back to London to attend to any outstanding business, it was on one of these trips on the 21st July 1969 that I watched the first Moon Landings on colour television in our lounge in Ley Street. Jean, who was still in Devon, could only watch it in black and white. Colour television only started broadcasting the year before initially in London. There were two television sets in our lounge: one to watch pictures in black and white, the other for colour which only received programmes from BBC2 for a couple of hours a day.

In White Car days, our family and friends enjoyed the comfort and ancient décor with its timber beams of the Black

Venus. I even treated my bank manager, Jimmy Rideout and a great friend (solicitor) Eddie to a long weekend there. We went horse riding one day and on another we walked across the moor, with steaks in the evening in the Inn's fine restaurant. Good for the soul and relaxation.

*Me enjoying a ride on Exmoor*

As an aside I will move on to the early eighties for a few paragraphs. We had lost touch with John when he remarried a few years after the above events. By then we had moved to Bristol. I had a business appointment in Cornwall and had decided to drive down the previous evening. It was a dark moonless night and I was travelling on the A30 the other side of Okehampton on a pitch black empty road, and a little hungry with no eateries in sight. A little further on in the distance there were some lights which turned out to be a pub. I thought maybe they do food, if not at least I will get a packet of crisps. I pulled into the almost deserted car park.

Behind the bar a tall sombre-looking man dressed formally in black, a touch of old castles and Dracula came to mind. We instantly recognised that we knew one another. As the conversation progressed it turned out he used to be the landlord of The Queens, a pub in Ilfracombe in Devon. John and I had visited on a few occasions as he was a long-time friend of Johns and had also been his best man when he married his first wife.

I said something like 'I had not seen or been in touch with John for about twelve years'. He replied, "You don't know then?" He paused looking at me and said, "I have just come back from his funeral." It turned out his liver finally gave up the fight.

What a coincidence to be on that road, which I rarely use, choose that pub on that particular night out of all the others on the two hundred mile journey to Cornwall. I left there slightly in shock and feeling a bit spooked.

\*\*

The Association and NRC Insurance Brokers grew out of the office in Hackney, and moved to larger premises in Woodford in East London. The walls were oak panelled with a carpeted floor. We also installed an internal telephone exchange system with a telephonist. In the rear office we had a very early type of computer to monitor payments from those who we insured on behalf of the insurer. It was a lot more comfortable to work in and far more impressive than the previous premises. It was a period when we were being treated royally, not only invitations to dinner and dances; I would also be invited to banker's dinners by the manager of White Cars bank, a real honour.

Our brokerage had its own bankers in the Strand in London and on occasion I would be invited there for lunch, in the very old superbly furnished Liberal Club, which was not too far from the bank, and where butlers wait on your every whim.

On another occasion, Michael invited me for tea with strawberries and cream on the terrace overlooking the River Thames at the House of Commons, which I went with pride as very few people have the opportunity so it is a real honour. He wanted me to meet a person in Government who was going to help in what we were trying to achieve for the trade. It makes you feel good when policemen salute you as you pass.

Life was perfect: a substantial sum of money on deposit in the bank, and in a period when most cars on the road were British made and a foreign vehicle was unusual, I drove the latest top of the range Volvo car and Jean used the 3 Litre Viscount. We took frequent holidays or long weekends abroad, which was not very common in the late sixties.

The Association was doing fine; I was travelling the country talking to members and trying to solve, on their behalf some of the problems they had, mainly with local authorities, and, of course, selling them insurance. A group of us went on a trade mission to Sweden to see how the car hire industry worked there.

I stayed in constant touch with Rowland, who was the Managing Director of Union Accident Insurance Company. We became good friends and we would meet on a regular basis and normally go out to lunch in a restaurant near his offices. He was very pleased with the way the brokerage was working, he also told me the level of claims was far lower than for normal car insurance.

It was early one morning when I arrived in my nicely decorated white carpeted office with teak furniture, the phone was ringing on the leather topped desk, and it was my friend with shocking news. The Board of Trade had given them one month's notice to increase their financial capital base if they were to continue offering insurance cover for motor vehicles, or they would lose their license to trade.

Suddenly the future did not look so good. I called Ron Williams at his base in South London where he operated a car hire company; as a convenience he could also issue cover notes to our clients on that side of the River Thames. I told him the bad news and that it was okay to continue with clients that were in the system but we could not issue new cover.

The news spread fast, national newspapers wanted to talk to me, and we had many drivers on the phone worried about their insurance cover, and of course they stopped paying their premiums, we were in a lot of difficulty.

# 1970s and the Triple Whammy

Things started to go downhill very quickly. The news of the decline of Union Accident had been well publicised in the media and on TV, drivers as stated started ringing worrying about their cover and companies were cancelling, obtaining insurance cover elsewhere.

Income dried up as we were not selling policies, but overheads still had to be met which put a drain on the bank and I was getting frantic calls from the manager who was asking what our intentions were.

I was on the phone most of the day arranging meetings with other insurance companies but the answer was always no, they did not believe that the scheme we were selling was profitable, especially as UA had been forced to stop trading. And yet the truth was we were the most profitable portfolio of the insurer with less claims per vehicle insured than any other.

At that time a new American based company set up offices in London called Cloverleaf. They intended selling motor insurance in a similar way to how we had been doing. I went and saw them and met the Managing director, a fellow called Dean White sitting behind a very large desk, so large you could have landed a helicopter on it, well alright then a small one − at the front edge his name on a large brass plate, this plaque was staring me in the face.

At that time Dean Martin was a very popular singer and this name plate was so large the name 'Dean' was in my eyes, as a result I kept calling him Mr Martin. It did not go down very well and he cut the meeting short by saying, "We do not need your members, shortly they will come to us anyway." I left with my tail between my legs.

Rowland and I spoke almost daily and two weeks had passed when he told me to stop looking for an alternative facility as he had someone lined up for us. At that time he was not prepared to say who, but if talks went as he expected he would arrange a meeting for us in a few days.

The days dragged by all the time wondering who and what the new facility would be. It could not have been better. Where I had been turned down as an *'up start'* in the insurance world Rowland had a long history in the industry. He also had, as Managing Director of the failed company figures to prove how sound, financially viable and profitable the insurance scheme was which we were running.

It was a few days later when Ron and I were in the City of London at the Lloyd's Insurance Building, where we were introduced to a Lloyd's broker who would act as the intermediary. We would carry on selling the insurance cover and he would place the risk with Lloyd's.

We were overwhelmed as the chance to sell Lloyd's of London insurance is a rare honour and only given to people after years in the industry, and what a lovely ´V´ sign to Mr Martin sorry, White. Lloyd's sent a team to our offices to inspect our facility, looking to see how we monitored payments and handled security because cover note books are very valuable and in the wrong hands can cause all sorts of problems. They were most impressed by the computer system for monitoring payments and our other facilities for operating the brokerage.

I touched on it earlier but it is important that I should explain why cover note books are so valuable. The document in them is proof of insurance, and in the case of motor vehicles very important as to drive without cover is illegal and very serious and one of the penalties is loss of your driving licence.

The pages in the books are in triplicate, the top sheet goes to the client, the next to the insurance company, the third kept in the book. All the sheets are numbered and in numerical order, when written out they are dated and timed, so each cover note must be dated after the previous one. But no matter how fraudulently the document was produced the insurance company in the event of an accident are still liable for any cost incurred.

What a difference the Lloyd's facility made, well established insurance brokers across the land had been trying to get a similar arrangement, and there we were with just a few years in the industry behind us riding high with the best insurance cover that could be offered anywhere.

We were being bombarded by other well-known names in the industry to allow them to sell the facility, the answer was always no, because I had other plans. I was also offered a six figure sum to sell the business to one broker, again I turned it down.

Rowland had another few months winding up Union Accidents affairs, and it was agreed that when he finally left there we would employ him and also he would be entitled to shares in the company. The plan, using his knowledge and contacts in the insurance world, would enable us to spread our facility into other types of cover beside private hire motor insurance. We also wanted to insure other types of vehicles, the possibilities were endless.

# INSURANCE BROKERS

*The Reliable Nationwide Insurance for Private Hire at Lloyds*

**Immediate Cover**

**Plus RADIO INSURANCE**

I did not see any harm in allowing Ron to have a cover note book in his office, we had a lot of clients south of the Thames, which was his part of London, so it made sense for people to be able to collect documents from his office.

We were very busy again, and when POB magazine was published with our advert, there was also a piece written in the financial pages of the Daily Mirror which helped to spread the word that we could offer solid vehicle cover through a name that was undisputed in the industry as the best, the phones did not stop ringing. Rowland finally joined us and we started to take the next step in our expansion, to sell house and building insurance cover. We formed a new company called Black Venus Ltd with fond memories of Devon. Through Rowland's contacts company representatives started to call vying for our business. We also started to advertise for normal car cover.

We agreed to do business with one of the companies and I was presented with a solid gold hallmarked Schaeffer ball point pen. This was before we had even sold any policies for them, which demonstrates the value of the business that was available to them and us. After the horror of the collapse of UA, and the fear of wondering how to survive, we were once more on a high, I was still driving the latest Volvo car, and all of our companies were doing well.

It was around this time that I was hospitalised with Renal Colic, a very bad pain in the kidneys. I was taken by ambulance to the hospital, and on arrival a person in a white coat was asking me questions, and I was getting impatient as all I wanted was something to take the pain away.

He asked had I been drinking and how much, in my frustration I answered a couple of bottles of Vodka and some brandies, I didn't think he would take me seriously, but he did and marked my records with a `D´ the doctors code for a drunk, and that is where it stayed until I discovered it years later. It took ten days before I was allowed home from hospital.

The hospital insisted on regular visits with a specialist as I still had a numbing pain. It was some time after that the consultant gave me a choice of either an operation or for him to prescribe a little yellow pill, likening it to what some diabetic people had to take insulin all their life. He said I had a chemical imbalance and these little pills would help to stop that discrepancy.

**

Ted Heath, the Conservative Prime Minister came into power in the early seventies and the opposition parties were not very happy, especially some of the more militant Trade Unions, mainly the miners. Most electricity power stations ran on coal-fired boilers and when the miners started taking strike action, the threat of power cuts became very real.

I saw an advertisement in a journal for small generators powered by a two stroke petrol engine. I was concerned − if as had been threatened we were going to have power cuts, because if there was not enough coal being mined to keep the power stations delivering power, then White Cars would have a problem. All our communication systems needed direct power to keep them operating. So I drove to West London and bought the generator.

People sniggered when I fitted it to the rear of the property and ran power wires through the ground floor to the control room − so in the event of a power cut we only needed to start the generator and change the electric plugs from the mains to our own supply, and we were back on air.

When the first blackout came and everywhere the lights went out and the whole area was in a deep gloom, White Cars stood out like a beacon and questions were being asked in the newspapers. 'Why did we have power when the rest of Ilford was in darkness?' There were also nasty letters in the press suggesting we had some influence in higher circles to be able to have lighting.

The argument with the miners dragged on, and there were more and more power cuts. Businesses started to suffer, and people were being laid off work, working days were cut to only three days a week and only then if there was enough power to run the factories and offices.

The car hire trade suffered badly, which also meant we were not selling as many insurance policies as previously, and I was disappointed that we had not gone into other types of insurance earlier. To help with our own private finances Jean returned to Lloyd's Bank, and was posted to Walthamstow branch where she started as a cashier.

People instead of hiring a car, were walking to work and they were not going to the pubs or clubs in the evening. Things were getting very difficult. By cutting back on expenditure we could survive, but we had to lay staff off and that was a very hard decision to make. With a small increase in the cost of the policies we were selling we were staying in profit and covering costs.

I was constantly feeling very tired, but we were under a lot of stress. The political situation was not improving, but I could not shake off the feeling of not being able to cope, not knowing at that time the little yellow pills the consultant had prescribed, and who said they were not a drug, but a chemical that my body was lacking. They were in fact Valium − a pill prescribed to slow people down and to remove stress.

The crash came very quickly and from a direction I never expected. It was early one morning I had arrived in the office as usual before any staff. The phone was ringing on my desk, I remember thinking that the last time it was ringing this early it was bad news, and it was, it was the Lloyd's broker, with the worst news.

They had received a copy cover note which had been back dated. I said that it was not possible as we checked every one. They said that this one had been sent to them in the post and not by way of our office. I was devastated, our facility was withdrawn immediately and with an illegal cover note being issued, no other insurer would come near us. NRC Insurance Brokers came to an end.

It was Ron Williams, when one of his vehicles had had an accident he discovered he had not renewed the insurance cover and the police wanted to see it. But by then he had already issued cover on another vehicle. So he did what is in the insurance world a big 'NO NO', he backdated a cover note to please the police officer, but in doing so destroyed everything we had been building, also a comfortable livelihood, both for him and us.

He knew exactly what he had done, by sending the false cover note directly in the post not to our office, where it would have been noticed; perhaps he thought it would not be checked by Lloyd's Underwriters.

There was nowhere to go, we lost everything, I became very ill; not only with the shock of the loss of a great business, but because of the drugs. It was many years before I got back on my feet and started again

# And After

It was not until five years later, in the early eighties, did doctors realise that Valium was a dangerous drug, by then we had moved to the West Country and were living near Bath. Dr. Peter Valentine our GP started to wean me off the tablets and after a period of sleepless nights and a load of support from Jean and my family I managed to dispense with them.

At one stage I was housebound with a terrible fear of open spaces; I spent some time in hospital in Bath, and that is where I started to write my first novel which was published in 1983. But before that date, on being discharged from the sickbay I carried on writing and trying to find work, eventually in 1981 I took a position on a commission only basis of selling kitchens. The firm I was working for had an architect's design department where I learned the trade of designing houses, extensions and the like.

I set up my own practice working from home, which became very successful, undertaking all types of work, I moved to offices in Bristol on a business park where I was employing four people. Jean was doing very well in the bank working her way up to management.

Various successful business ventures later, lead to our retirement and the chance to write further. Further became further afield when we moved to Spain in the year 2000 where we live in the mountains forty minutes drive from the Costa

Blanca Coast. We have a five bedroom house which we let out to holiday makers and it keeps us very busy, but I still find time to write.

Percy W Chattey
percy@fuentelargo.com
www.percychatteybooks.com

In the following pages the opening
Foreword to Percy's novel,
*The Black Venus*, which is now available through Kindle
and Amazon.


The Black Venus

*Authors note: Calling this book 'The Black Venus', is in
some ways to honour the memory of a great friend, John
Green, who in the 1960s bought an old drinking house on
Exmoor, in the village of Challacombe in Devon. He renamed
it from 'The Ring of Bells' to 'The Black Venus' after seeing a
reference to the name in the history of the four hundred year
old property. He also turned it into a small guest house in the
wonderful setting of this tiny village on the moors. At that time
my wife Jean, and I, were great friends with him and spent
many a happy hour in his company and the comfort of the Inn.*

*The Black Venus still exists today and in no way is this
book any reference to it and the tales told here are purely
imaginative.* **Before the story itself** *I thought it may be fun to
imagine how the name came about. For 'Venus' in Roman
mythology means 'God of Love' – so why Black?*


## *A Dark Night early spring 1649*

The twin mast schooner battled its way through the heavy
swell of the waters off the south coast of England as it headed
for the small inlet, known as The Venus Cove. The cove a
wide deep water opening in the coastline was large enough to
allow the keel of the sailing ship to pass safely over the mud
below and anchor safely. The Captain had sailed into this small
waterway many times and was aware of its many dangers. To
the bow of the ship the navigating officer was casting a knotted
line forward over the bow measuring the depth of the water
whilst the master was shouting orders to the sailors controlling

the rigging, to lower the sails, so that the ship would slow to an acceptable forward movement.

To one side stranded on the mud banks were the remains of a smaller vessel than the one now navigating into the small cove. He, the captain, had known the senior officer and most of the crew and had seen them as friends of what was now little more than an empty wreck. That was all before the ill fated night the ship was steered too close to the shore never to leave it again. When the King's Revenue Men arrived accompanied by soldiers on horseback, the crew, who were smuggling barrels of wine were caught red-handed and following a brief fight the poorly equipped sailors were overwhelmed and those not killed were taken for trial. The grounded vessel relieved of its stock was left to rot.

Over the years the old craft had been vandalised and most of her fittings had been removed. Some of the timbers of the stricken vessel had been stripped for use on other ships, in other instances materials to help build the small houses where the local fishermen lived. One part of the wreck remained because of superstition and the bringing of bad luck. That part was the carved coloured figurehead at the bow, of a lady in flight − her arms outstretched with the name Venus below her, the name of the old timber built ship, and the name the small inlet was to become known by.

The crewmen were rushing around the wooden decks preparing ropes to be used to secure the craft in the small bay when it came to rest. Another team were releasing ropes securing barrels and crates tied firmly to the decks, moving them to the edge where they could be off offloaded on to small rowing boats which were coming out from the shore to meet the newcomer.

The shore men, a lot earlier in the day had posted lookouts high in the hills above the inlet. Others were patrolling the small lanes around the area fearful of the Revenue men. The small boats from the shore were tying up alongside the new arrival. From the decks the burly sailors were lowering the kegs of spirit to handlers in the smaller craft and when full they pushed away from the ship. These little boats heavily laden, the water lapping at the gunnels, were propelled by oarsmen to the small wooden landing stage where a line of donkeys were waiting, each with bags of wool to be illegally exported.

Once the barrels from the ship had been transferred to the shore where the animals had waited patiently and the bales of wool were loaded in return, it was time for the vessel to put to sea. The unloading and the exporting of the other goods had taken longer than expected and Captain knew he had been longer than he wished to be in the small cove and was anxious to get moving away from the area. On shore another group of men lead the donkeys, now laden with a barrel to each flank, up the gravel surfaced path away from the deep water inlet.

As they approached the end of the cove, the path became steeper, the surface rutted and not very firm under foot as it followed the small river that flowed into the bay. A little further on the path was becoming very steep and where the water fell over rocks from the higher ground, a waterfall formed as the water cascaded down the incline and foaming as it reached the bottom. The men leading the donkeys needed to encourage them by pulling them and pushing them up the gradient.

They followed the river nestling in the valley between the woodlands of the surrounding hills. As the sun started to appear over the horizon the smugglers made camp and lightened the loads on the animals settling down and waiting for the cover of darkness before continuing their journey inland to the small inn. Here their goods would be collected; in return they would receive payment for their work. After which, with nothing more to do, they would wait for news of the arrival of another vessel.

The Inn was really only a small bar where they were heading, although only a few miles in from the sea, it would take the men with the donkeys more than two nights to reach it. The first sighting for them as they came over the brow of a hill was to see it settling in a small hamlet next to the river that they had been following. It was surrounded by tall old oak trees, their branches shading the stone built bar, which was the largest building in this small group of dwellings, used not only for merriment but also as a place where the community could meet.

The old oak panelled door with a crude handwritten sign above it declaring it to be 'The Venus', itself named after the rotting craft way down in the bay, where some of the fittings and timbers had been used to build the bar. The four smugglers pushed open the door and entered the stone built room, a long open area with a dirt floor and a ceiling so low they had to bow their heads. Fixed into small alcoves in the walls oil lamps gave off a yellow light which cast eerie shadows around the walls.

To one end a log fire blazed in the grate of the large fireplace with stone seats built into the walls to its sides where on cold nights people could sit out of the draughts in the room. At the opposite end was a long table which acted as the bar. The owner, a lady in her thirties, wore a flared skirt which dragged on the floor at her feet. It was she who now ran 'The Venus' after losing her husband to the dreaded disease of smallpox a few years before.

The four men were given a warm welcome by the merry makers in the room and jugs of ale were put before them which they quickly swallowed. A regular customer known for his musical and singing skills bent over from the chair where he was sitting and lifted a string instrument on to his lap and started strumming as he sang a popular melody, the people around him clapping in time.

A short time later having quenched their thirst, the band of men went outside to unload the animals carrying the contraband goods into the stone built store. The dark grey thatched roof was a striking contrast to the clay red tiles of the bar.

The merriment and celebrations went on late into the night. A few women came from their small cottages to help with the laughter and in some cases to help husbands and boyfriends home to a blissful night of deep sleep in their drunkenness.

It had been a lot earlier when by chance two Revenue Men, whose job it was to patrol the area, had seen the line of donkeys making their way along a little used footpath to the hamlet. They had dismounted from their steeds and while one kept the horses quiet the other followed the line of animals and men making sure of their destination. Convinced they had not been seen they rode off to get support from a garrison of soldiers to arrest the men and the people in the small village who were involved in this Capital Crime against the King.

Not many of the revellers heard the sound of the troops coming as they galloped along the poor roads leading to the hamlet. A few who heard the noise of the hooves pounding the ground sat up where they were sleeping. Horror in their minds as they remembered what happened to smugglers when caught; leaping from their beds and escaping into the surrounding countryside. Others were not quick enough and stood their ground drawing swords to fight off the intruding forces, the drink and lack of sleep hindered their chances of fighting off the King's Men, and those that resisted arrest were killed where they stood. The Revenue Men were more interested in the bar and its contents; they had brought two wagons with them each drawn by two strong horses to confiscate the merchandise.

They marched into the bar searching cupboards, turning over tables, in their search for the illegal goods. In the small room at the back they found the landlady. She was cuddled up to one of the smugglers. The man tried to put up a fight but the Revenue Man shot him with a pistol musket he pulled from his belt.

Two of the heavily built men dragged the owner from her bed pulling the screaming woman into the bar, her feet dragging on the dirt floor; sitting her down they tied her to a chair. Making sure she was secure they left her while they went outside to count the barrels and to supervise the loading of the wagons.

The soldiers had rounded up some of the men and women who had not escaped. They were lined up with their arms tied behind their backs, the ropes cutting into their skin as they were all linked together in a line.

The Revenue men who had been trying for some time to find the source of the contraband goods which had been entering the area, and being sold far and wide, sat to one side to work out what the next step was to be. They were determined to stop this smuggling racket. From the group, four of them, two more had joined when the original two had gone for reinforcements, three wanted to destroy the small village there and then. The fourth argued that they should arrest them and take them into the Garrison town of Houghton, where they would be tried in a court. The three got their way and they decided to hold the court straight away.

With the owner still tied and sitting on the chair they formed a circle sitting on benches in front of her. They explained they worked for and represented the King of the land and they had the authority to stamp out all activities concerning smuggling. The hearing only took a few minutes, after which they took her outside put her on a horse with a rope around her neck tied to the oak tree. The horse was whipped across its flanks from which it bolted. The owner of The Venus was left hanging.

The soldiers marched the remainder of the people away, leaving the small village empty and left to the wilds of nature.

In the course of time the bar reopened, a new road had been built from the town of Houghton by a business man who saw the opportunity of developing the small bay. The old stone bar would be on the new route and the new occupier developed it, the old sign was still hanging above the door but knowing something of its history, he changed the name and called it The Black Venus.

**\*\***

**The above is the Author's imagination of how the small inn on Exmoor got its name.**

*The Black Venus is a story of love, murder and revenge. How did a civil war in the Balkans result in murder in a small community in Southern England? Revenge, how were the Irish involved? Above all of the horror, there is the love and passion of two people.*

*A book that you will not want to put down, available from Amazon, Kindle and other outlets.*

*Percy's new novel 'Death for a Starter' is set in the eighteen hundreds and tells the story of one family's battle against the potato famine in Ireland and their flight to England and how their lives changed.*